THE JUDAS TRAP

When her 'friend' Diane Tregower
tricked her into going to Cornwall and
confronting Michael Tregower, Sara
Fortune could have found herself in a
very unpleasant and dangerous situation
indeed—but instead she and Michael
fell in love and all could have ended
happily. Had it not been for the secret
that Sara dared not tell him . . .

Books you will enjoy
by ANNE MATHER

MELTING FIRE

Olivia owed her stepbrother Richard a lot—
no doubt about that. But did that give him the
right to declare that he owned her, that what
she did with her life was for him to decide?
Olivia had to admit that she was becoming
more and more reluctant to tear herself away
from him—yet if she didn't, how was she ever
going to have any life or experience of her own?

FALLEN ANGEL

Jason Tarrant hadn't wanted a teenage ward
wished on to him—and he wanted it even less
when the boy he had expected turned out to be
a girl; an *estancia* in South America was hardly
the place for someone like Alex Durham. And
when Alex, in her artless way, began to throw
herself at his head the situation looked like
getting out of hand . ...

CAPTIVE DESTINY

Eight years ago, Emma and Jordan had been
wildly in love—but then suddenly Jordan's
attitude had changed and he had thrown her
out of his life. Now he had come back again,
saying he still loved her—but what could she
do about it? For now she was married to David,
who had more claim to her loyalty than
Jordan ever would . . .

FOLLOW THY DESIRE

On the day of her wedding, Helen realised that
she could not go through with it—not now that
she had met Barry's half-brother Morgan. So
instead she accepted Morgan's invitation to
go back with him to Africa to look after his
young daughter. But Morgan had not mentioned marriage, and in fact had made it clear
that the job was all he was offering her. Was
Helen making a complete fool of herself—or
worse?

THE JUDAS TRAP

BY

ANNE MATHER

MILLS & BOON LIMITED
17–19 FOLEY STREET
LONDON W1A 1DR

First published 1979
Australian copyright 1979
Philippine copyright 1979
This edition 1979

© Anne Mather 1979

ISBN 0 263 73106 5

Set in Linotype Baskerville 10 on 11½ pt.

Made and printed in Great Britain by
Richard Clay (The Chaucer Press), Ltd., Bungay, Suffolk

CHAPTER ONE

IT was certainly remote—Diane had been right about that. Remote and unfamiliar, and undeniably beautiful. In spite of the narrow roads and the high hedges, which gave her a claustrophobic feeling at times, the glimpses of the ocean she saw below the headland were as wild and as blue as she could have imagined. When she opened the car window the air smelt unmistakably of salt, but it was still chilly, and she was glad to close it again.

Sara had never been to Cornwall before; in fact, she had never been further west than Bristol. She had spent her holidays in Spain and Italy, the certainty of good weather inspiring more enthusiasm than the tourist resorts of her own country. Besides, she had never cared for those regular pictures of bumper-to-bumper traffic streaming into the West Country on every Bank and public holiday. Instead, she had gone abroad to some equally busy spot, the difference being that she could complete her journey in one easy stage —and avoid over-excitement.

This was different. This was escape. And she was fast learning there was still a part of England where the demands of the automobile did not hold sway. The villages she had passed did not cater to the tourist's needs, nor did they seek to detain the passing motorist. On the contrary, she had felt a sense of intrusion, of being a trespasser into a world where she was the inter-

loper, a strangely alien world that was as remote from
London as it was possible to be.

It was strange to think that Diane Tregower had
been born here, not in this particular spot, but in Falmouth, which was not so many miles away. Who would
have dreamed that the daughter of a fisherman could
aspire to such heights, could leave the quiet harbour
town where she had grown to womanhood, and become one of the most sought-after actresses on the London stage? It was unusual, and unexpected, but life was
sometimes like that. Her husband must have cursed
the day he invited the famous producer Lance Wilmer,
filming in the area, to dinner at Ravens Mill, and set
in motion the events which were to end so disastrously.

Sara shivered. Poor Adam! He must have gone
through hell knowing what Diane and Lance had become to one another, and then losing his sight like
that ... It was terrible, and humiliating somehow, recalling his eventual reconciliation to their affair, and
his subsequent plea to Diane to continue to regard
Ravens Mill as her home.

Not that she had ever taken him up on it. In the
seven years since their separation she had seen him
only once, and that was when he was in hospital, re-
covering from the accident which robbed him of his
sight. She might not have seen him then, but Lance
had insisted on it, Diane had told Sara, relating what
a story it had made for the press.

'It was quite a poignant little scene,' she had said,
with a slight curl to her lips, and Sara had marvelled
that anyone who could portray such convincing emotion in public should in reality feel so little. Diane had
no real sympathy, no compassion for the man she had
married when she was sixteen and left without a qualm

five years later, and it was doubtful whether her involve-
ment with Lance Wilmer was anything more than a
means to an end. Diane was ambitious, she had always
been ambitious, and an innate aptitude for mimicry
with a natural ability to act had given her the confidence she needed. The fact that she was also a very
beautiful woman in no way detracted from the undoubted talent she possessed, and with Wilmer's backing she had been an immediate success.

Sara's slim fingers felt clammy against the steering
wheel as a signpost warned her that the miles between
herself and Ravens Mill had narrowed to single figures.
Calm down, she thought. It's only a house. A nice
house with, according to Diane, a magnificent view of
the Atlantic Ocean. A lonely house, a quiet house, a
retreat, where she could go and soothe her own shattered emotions, sure in the knowledge that no one who
knew her would guess where she had gone.

It had been Diane's idea, of course. The house was
standing empty, she said, virtually unused, Adam having abandoned his lonely vigil years ago to live in a
warmer climate. He had inherited a villa in Portugal,
she had explained vaguely, not specifying why or from
whom, and since the Tregowers, like everyone else,
were feeling the pinch, it was cheaper and easier to live
out of the country.

Sara knew that the Tregowers had once been a
wealthy family. Their money had financed the now-
crumbling tin mines, and compared to Diane's lot as
the eldest daughter in a family of seven children, marriage to Adam Tregower had been quite an achieve-
ment. Sara could only assume that the man had been
dazzled by Diane's beauty, for he had been more than
ten years older than she was, and obviously more

sophisticated. But marry her he had, and as his own
parents were dead there had been no one to offer any
objections.

The road was winding round the headland now, and
below the labouring engine of the Mini the ground fell
away to the ragged rocks that scarred the coastline.
Surging white foam gave a lacy illusion of innocence
to jagged crags which, as the tide fell away, revealed
themselves as savage denizens of this wild and beautiful
shore. It was bleak and desolate, cruel even, but its very
isolation appealed to Sara's mood. Diane had been
right when she said she could find release here, away
from the rough and tumble of everyday living, and
Sara was grateful for whatever grain of compassion had
compelled the woman to offer her the house for the
two weeks she could afford to stay.

Sara's relationship with Diane Tregower was a
curious one. As an editor in a small publishing house,
she had few opportunities to meet members of the
theatre world, but Lance Wilmer was her father's
cousin, and occasionally, if he needed an extra guest
for his dinner parties, he invited Sara along to make
up the numbers. It was on one such occasion, at the
beginning of their relationship, that Sara had been
introduced to Diane Tregower.

From the start Diane had been attracted to her. The
fact that Sara's blonde good looks had appeared like a
pale copy of herself might have had something to do
with it, or maybe her weakness had aroused her sympathy, or perhaps at that time Diane had been feeling
a little unsure of herself, and Sara's evident admiration
had been a salve to her ego. Whatever the reasons,
they had become friends, and Sara, seven years her
junior, became her sometimes unwilling confidante.

Yet for all that, she was fond of Diane, although her attempts to interfere with Sara's life were not always welcome. Even so, it was Diane who had revealed Tony in his true colours, and Diane who had arranged for her to get away on her own for a while ...

Her jaw shook for a moment at the remembrance of that particular revelation. She had not been able to believe it at first. Tony had seemed so sure of himself, of his love for her, he had told her so a dozen times. They had even discussed getting married. But then Diane had accidentally mentioned that Sara had a heart condition, and Tony had started finding excuses why they could not meet ...

A few drops of rain speckled the windscreen, and determinedly she thrust her disturbing thoughts aside and concentrated on the road ahead. They were descending now, a hazardous hairpin descent towards a cluster of cottages that appeared to be clinging to the cliff-face above a rocky inlet. Nearer, she could see a harbour wall, and fishing boats drawn within its sheltering arm, and then the road was ascending again towards a headland where, through the now driving rain, she could see a house standing alone and unguarded.

It had to be Ravens Mill, she realised, the thought banishing her earlier depression from her mind. Diane had described the area in some detail, and it fitted exactly her description of bleakness and isolation. What Diane had not told her was its size, and its formidable appearance, and she gazed in trepidation at the stark stone walls that rose above her.

A stone gateway gave access to a weed-strewn drive that had to lead to the house, and pulling her mouth down at the corners, Sara stood on her brakes. This

wasn't the sort of place one could spend a couple of
weeks in privacy, this was no country cottage where one
might regain one's peace of mind, she thought in dismay. It was a country seat, a family pile, the kind of
place where half a dozen servants were needed just to
keep down the dust. Diane had given her her key, and
picturing a house of reasonable proportions, Sara had
equipped herself with a sleeping bag for using until she
had tidied the place out and aired bedding, etc., but
that seemed ludicrous now. Diane had said a Mrs Penworthy came in now and then to open windows and
so on, but sitting there, Sara began to doubt the truth
of that statement. Did one open up such a place, just
for airing? Could one? There would be so many rooms
—reception rooms, sitting rooms, dining rooms, bed-
rooms ...

Hunching her shoulders, she looked at the square
masculine watch on her narrow wrist. It was already
after five. It would be dark in a couple of hours, and
although she did not look forward to driving back to
the nearest town over those roads in this weather, the
prospect of spending the night alone in this gloomy
mansion did not appeal.

Glancing behind her, she surveyed the pile of
baggage that overloaded the back seat of the Mini and
spilled on to the floor. As well as her sleeping bag and
pillows there were suitcases containing her clothes,
fresh linen and food enough for a couple of days—and
the briefcase containing the first draft of her novel.
Compressing her lips, she sighed. The book—it was an
adventure story for children—needed a lot of work,
but in her professional opinion it had the makings of
a publishable novel. She had planned to re-write it
during these unexpected weeks of freedom. It had
been her goal and, she hoped, her salvation, and maybe,

with a published book behind her, she would have more confidence in herself and her future.

She shifted round again in her seat. If she left now, she would never re-write the book: she was sure of that. Back in London, work would overtake her, no matter how understanding her boss had been in allowing her to take her holiday so early, and there was always the possibility that she would give in to phoning Tony again and lose what little self-respect she had.

The storm suddenly dispersed as quickly as it had appeared, and a watery sun filtered through the clouds. April showers, thought Sara wryly, watching the amber rays strike gold on blank panes. The upper floors of the house were visible between the yews that marked the drive, and on impulse she decided to take a look. After all, it was foolish coming all this way without even venturing inside, and now that the sun had come out its aspect was so much less forbidding. On the contrary, Sara could see that with care and attention Ravens Mill could become a most attractive dwelling place, and she could well imagine Diane's sense of triumph when she first became mistress of the house.

The drive had a slight curve that successfully cut off any prying eyes from the road, but the lodge that stood at its gates was unoccupied. Someone, perhaps the boys from the village, had broken several of the windows in the lodge, but so far the house seemed to have avoided accident.

The gravel of the drive itself sprouted weeds and crab grass, and the yews, left untended, had lost all shape and design. The lawns, that had once swept to the edge of the cliff itself, were no less neglected, and only a scythe would make any impression on such rampant vegetation.

Blinds were drawn at all the windows at the front of

the house, and Sara thought, rather imaginatively, that it seemed to be presenting a guarded face to the world. It was a shame that no one could afford to live here any more, she reflected, wondering if there was anything more melancholy than an empty house.

She stopped the Mini, switched off the engine, and climbed out. Immediately the chill wind off the ocean caught her breath, and she quickly reached into the car for the jacket of her jersey pants suit which she had discarded during the journey. Pulling it on over the matching brown silk shirt, she was glad of its high collar and the warmth it engendered as she rummaged in her handbag for the key Diane had given her.

The heavy studded door swung inward surprisingly easily on its hinges as she inserted the key, with none of the creaking and groaning she had been expecting. Half smiling at her own ghoulish imagination, she saw with relief that the sun was filtering through the blinds that shuttered the windows on either side of the door, and she was able to close it against the elements without fear of being unable to see. Nevertheless, she opened one of the blinds as soon as the door was shut, and looked about her with less confidence than curiosity.

She was standing in the hall of the house, she saw, with an enormously high ceiling arching away above her head. Directly ahead of her, twin staircases curved to a central flight that rose to the first floor, and in the dust-moted shafts of sunlight she could see the square portrait of a man that faced the first floor landing. To right and left, closed doors indicated the sitting rooms and drawing rooms that Sara had envisaged, while in the well of the stairs, a square oak chest shone with the patina of years. *Shone* ...

Sara's eyes widened, then she blinked. She had not really noticed before, but now she came to think of it, the place was surprisingly clean considering that no one was living there. Looking down at the polished wooden floor at her feet, strewn with rugs in a variety of shades and colours, she realised it, too, was well polished, and the faint smell that rose to her nostrils was that of beeswax.

A sense of unease rose inside her. Either Mrs Penworthy was as worthy as her name suggested, or Diane was wrong about the house being uninhabited. What if Adam, like his wife, had offered the place to a friend? What if right now, the present inhabitants of the house were out for the afternoon, visiting other friends or shopping ...

Her immediate impulse to flee was stifled. Surely if anyone was living in the house, they would have opened the blinds? Besides, wouldn't Diane have known if her husband was back in England? She wouldn't have sent her, Sara, down here if there was the remotest chance that Adam was back in the country, would she?

Her heart slowing its quickened beat a little, she tried to think coherently. After all, Diane had known she was coming down here, and what more natural but that she should ask this Mrs Penworthy, whoever she was, to come in and tidy round in readiness? Surely that was the only explanation, and justification in fact for her decision to come and investigate. If she had turned round and left without even entering the building, she would never have known the trouble that lady had gone to on her behalf, and she assured herself that she ought to be honoured to be treated in this way. A wave of warmth towards Diane engulfed her. It had been kind of her to go to all this trouble. Uncharacteristically so, remembering the callous way she had denounced Tony's behaviour. How could she in all conscience turn it down?

'So you came, Diane!'

The deep masculine voice that riveted her to the spot came from an opened doorway to the right of the hall. It was a leather-studded door, the kind of door that indicated its usage beyond, and until that moment had scarcely imprinted itself on Sara's mind. A library, or a study, she had registered in passing, and moved on to other things.

But now the door stood wide, and a man was standing in the aperture, the dim light behind him hardly illuminating his still form. A tall man, with a lean body, and straight dark hair that fell smoothly across his forehead. His features were vaguely distinguishable—high cheekbones, a prominent nose, a thin-lipped mouth—but it was not these characteristics she recognised. She had seen pictures of Adam Tregower, and she had no doubt that this was he, but it was his motionlessness that identified him to her—that, and the dark glasses he wore, and the drawn blinds behind him. What would a blind man want with sunlight?

His words were less easy to interpret. *So you came, Diane!* What did it mean? What did *he* mean? Had he sent for his wife? Had he contacted Diane and asked to see her? Asked her to come down here, in fact?

Sara's heart pounded unevenly. Her immediate impulse to deny the identity he had placed upon her was silenced by a feeling of intrusion, an invasion into this man's privacy that she had had no right to make. It was not herself who should be standing here, but Diane, and to deny the truth of that statement was to tear aside Adam Tregower's self-respect. How could she tell him that Diane had sent her here? How could she admit to being an unwilling tool in some game Diane was playing, for as the minutes passed she became more and more convinced that the other girl had known her husband was waiting at the house.

Yet, equally, how could she not deny it? This man had been married to Diane for five years. He must know her face, the sound of her voice. But Adam Tregower was blind now, a victim of his own despair, and it was seven years since they had lived together ...

'Diane ...'

The man spoke again, and Sara stared helplessly in his direction. She had to speak, she had to answer him. Dear God, what did Diane expect of her?

'Adam?' she breathed tentatively, and she heard his sigh of relief. 'I—how are you?'

'How do I look?'

Evidently her husky tones were unidentifiable, and a trembling breath escaped her. What ought she to do? Denounce herself here and now, or tread deeper into this mire of deception? Adam Tregower had suffered so much. Could she honestly prevent him from suffering more? Why had he sent for Diane? Why did he want to speak to her? And why hadn't Diane told her?

Anger gripped her. Diane had known her husband was here: she was convinced of that now. So many small things were falling into place, not least the obvious one of Diane's suggestion that she should spend a couple of weeks at the house, a house she had taken care never to describe, so that Sara had expected something entirely different. Diane had known Adam was here, had known he was expecting his wife—and had sent her in her place, knowing that in her own grief, her sympathies would respond to this man's helplessness.

'You—you look well,' she got out now, although she could hardly tell his colouring in this half light. 'Adam, I——'

'It was good of you to come.' His words interrupted any explanation she might have hoped to make, and there was a curiously ironic note to his voice. 'I wonderd if you would. You lead such a—busy life. So different from my own.'

Sara's mouth was dry. Outside, she saw with alarm, the clouds were gathering once more, and even as her eyes darted to the blind she had drawn, a few drops of rain spattered the window. All of a sudden the precariousness of her position seemed untenable, and she took an involuntary step backward.

'Please.' As if aware of her panic, Adam Tregower stepped forward, moving surely across the hall towards her. 'Won't you come into the library? We can have a drink together before dinner, and it's easier to talk in less formal circumstances.'

'Oh, but . . .' Sara cast another longing look towards the windows. She couldn't stay here, she thought wildly, but how could she get away without proving that Diane had made a fool of him yet again? Maybe he did not expect her to stay. Surely he knew Diane would never agree to remain at the house, alone with him. Perhaps his invitation was for dinner only, a chance for them to talk together about—about—*what*? Old times? Hardly. Her work? Hardly that either. A divorce? She breathed wore freely. Yes, perhaps that was it. Adam wanted a divorce. He might have found someone else, someone he wanted to marry. A Portuguese girl maybe. A biddable Portuguese *dona da casa*, with no desire to do anything but care for her husband and bring up his children.

'Diane.'

He was closer now, and in the shaft of light issuing through the unguarded window she saw his eyes, shadowed behind the tinted lenses of his glasses. Deeply set eyes they were, beneath heavy lids, strangely piercing eyes that while she knew could not see her, seemed to penetrate her guilty façade. His face, too, was deeply tanned, evidence of the warmer climes he had been inhabiting, and his throat rising from the opened neckline of a dark blue shirt was strong and corded with muscle. There was a disc suspended from a gold chain about his throat, one of those coins that could be used as a means of identity, and he wore two rings, a plain gold signet ring, and a flat copper amulet. Although he resembled the pictures she had seen of Adam Tregower, in the flesh he seemed so much more disturbing somehow, and she began to understand why Diane had been so eager to become his wife. She wondered at the ambition which had driven the other girl to leave him, for while Lance Wilmer was a handsome man, he had never possessed this man's purely sexual attraction.

'Come . . .'

He was holding out a hand towards her now, and avoiding it she had no choice but to cross the hall towards the library door. There was a moment's pause before he followed her, and then she heard his footsteps right behind her.

The library was large, by anybody's standards, but age and neglect had added an air of dampness and decay. Nevertheless, a fire was smouldering comfortingly in the grate, and the smell of Havana tobacco went a long way to disguising its less pleasurable as-

pects. Shelves of books lined two long walls and half
the third, where drawn blinds indicated a shaded window. The fourth was taken up by the huge fireplace,
and a pair of darkwood cabinets, in which resided a
collection of chess pieces, from jade and ivory, to ebony
and alabaster. There was a desk, on which a tray of
drinks rested, and as well as the leather chair that
faced it there was a pair of worn green velvet armchairs that fronted one another across the hearth.

Hovering in the centre of the room, Sara heard
Adam close the door behind him, and presently he
passed her to indicate the chairs beside the fire.

'Won't you sit down?' he suggested, and with a sure-
ness born of long practice, his hand sought the tray of
drinks upon the desk.

Sara sat, partly because her legs felt a little unsure,
and partly because it put more distance between them.
It was all very well, posing as Caesar's wife, but she did
not know what he might expect of her, what indeed he
might do to induce her to stay.

The temptation to confess her identity rose within
her again only to be squashed as she watched him
fumbling with the bottles. Evidently their shape and
size identified them to him, and presently he turned
and said: 'What can I offer you? Whisky, gin? Or your
usual?' His lips twisted suddenly, the first sign of bitterness? 'Or perhaps it's not your usual any more.'

Sara hesitated. Diane's usual drink these days was
bitter lemon, with an occasional dash of vermouth,
when calories permitted.

'My—usual, I think,' she conceded doubtfully, and
swallowed rather convulsively when he presented her
with a tall glass that looked as if it contained Coke, and
smelled strongly of rum. She guessed Bacardi had been

added, and when she tasted it her suspicions were
justified.

'Ah ...' Adam had poured himself a measure of
whisky, holding the neck of the bottle against the rim
of the glass, listening to the sound it made and measur-
ing its contents accordingly. 'It's been a long time,
Diane.'

Sara nodded, realised he couldn't see her, and said:
'Yes,' in a low tone.

'I must say you're less—aggressive than I would have
expected,' he continued, surprisingly, supporting himself against the lip of the desk. 'I guessed you'd come—
but not without protest.'

Sara took a sip of her drink to give herself courage.
So it was confirmed. Adam had sent for Diane. But
why? Had he told her?

'Do you think the place has changed much?' he was
asking now, and as this was safer ground she felt able
to answer him.

'I think—there's dampness,' she ventured. 'I expect,
because the house has stood empty for so long ...'

'So long,' he agreed, his mouth drawing down at the
corners. 'Too long. What do you think, Diane?'

She didn't understand what he was getting at. Why
had he asked Diane to come down here? What possible
motive could he have? He must know she was a working actress—he had intimated as much in the hall. And
yet he thought he had persuaded her to come down
here ...

Sara pressed her lips together and stared anxiously
up at those hooded eyes, dark behind their concealing
lenses. What thoughts were going through his mind?
What manner of man was he to imagine he could
summon back a wife who had left him without scruple

seven years before? If, sick and blinded, after the accident when it was suspected he had tried to kill himself,
he had been unable to sustain Diane's sympathy, why
should he suppose she might come back now?

It was all getting rather deep and disturbing, and
with the sky darkening outside, Sara was feeling a
distinct sense of unease. It wasn't just that she was here
under false pretences. If she had been Diane herself,
she felt sure she would have experienced the same kind
of feeling, a sense of enclosure, of being trapped, of being imprisoned with this man in the darkness he had
occupied for the past seven years ...

'Another drink?' he suggested, but looking down at
the almost untouched glass in her hands Sara de-
murred.

'I—I shall have to be going soon,' she murmured,
and sensed rather than saw his stiffening features. 'I—
can't stay here.'

'Why not?' His voice was harsh. 'There are plenty
of rooms; *plenty*, as you know only too well.'

Sara set down her glass on the hearth, welcoming
the fire's warmth against her chilled fingers. 'I—I don't
think you understand'—she was beginning, deciding
this had gone far enough, when once again he interrupted her.

'It's you who don't understand, Diane!' he declared
coldly. 'I didn't bring you here for a friendly chat, as
you're aware. Nor do I intend that you should leave
again, the minute you decide I'm no real threat to that
comfortable life you've made for yourself!' He tossed
back the remainder of the whisky in his glass with a
careless gesture. Then he faced her across the width of
the faded patterned carpet, and if she had not known
better she would have sworn he could see her there,

sitting nervously on the edge of her chair. 'You came because my letter frightened you, because you didn't really believe it, but you couldn't be absolutely certain. Since your arrival you've been watching me, studying my reactions, trying to decide whether I meant what I said, and if I did, what I could do about it.'

Sara got to her feet jerkily. 'You don't understand, Mr Tregower,' she said then, fear combining with a natural nervousness to bring a tremor to her voice. 'I— I am not—not your wife, not Diane Tregower. My— my name is—is Sara Fortune, and—and I don't know what you're talking about.'

There was silence for several pregnant minutes, minutes when she could see he was grappling with what she had just said, digesting it, dissecting it, testing it for flaws, and finding it wanting. Then a bitter smile twisted his lips and a short harsh laugh broke from them.

'Oh, bravo, Diane, bravo!' he complimented her mockingly. 'Yes. Yes, indeed, that was worthy of the actress you undoubtedly are. To deny your own identity—how clever, and how apt! How could a blind man be sure you are who you say you are, particularly a blind man who has not seen you for so many years? The voice, the body, even the make-up of the face could have changed in that time. And he would have no way of knowing, no way of really being sure . . .'

Sara gasped. 'It's true. I'm not lying. I really am who I say I am.'

'Then why did you not say so before?'

'Why, I—because I——'

'Because you didn't think of it!'

'No!'

'Oh, come on . . .' There was nothing to pity about

him now. Standing squarely between her and the
door, he epitomised the dominant male, hard and
masculine, and totally without sympathy. 'I know you,
Diane. I know everything about you. I've listened, until
I'm sick to my teeth, to stories about your charm, your
looks, your likes, your dislikes, your absorption with
self, self, self ...'

'No!'

'I've watched a man disintegrate before my eyes, lose
all his confidence, his self-respect, even his will to live,
while he spoke of your needs, your demands, your success. Your *selfishness*, more like, your flawed image,
your destructive self-indulgence that must be satisfied,
whatever the cost!'

Sara didn't understand all of this. 'You—you
watched a man ...' she whispered unsteadily, and with
a savage oath he tore off the glasses which had concealed his eyes, revealing them to be a brilliant shade
of amber, burning now with the hard light of malevo-
lence.

'Oh, yes,' he said, as she stood there staring uneasily
at him, realising weakly that he could see. And why
not? This was *not* Adam Tregower—she realised that
now. The resemblance was there, the features followed
a similar pattern, and given the half light she could be
forgiven for mistaking his identity. But this man's face
was harder, stronger—younger. A relative, no doubt,
but not Diane's husband.

'You—you're not——' she stammered, wondering
why the knowledge gave her no relief, and he nodded.

'No, I'm not,' he agreed harshly. 'I'm Michael Tregower. Adam is—*was*—my brother!'

CHAPTER TWO

'You look shocked!' he declared a few moments later, as Sara continued to stare disbelievingly at him. 'Didn't you know Adam had a brother? Perhaps not. It doesn't surprise me. I was always considered the skeleton in the Tregower family cupboard.'

Sara licked her dry lips. 'Adam—Adam did not have a brother,' she declared, faintly but succinctly. 'I know. Di—Diane told me.'

'Really.' Plainly he did not believe the latter half of her statement. 'Well, I'm sorry to disappoint you, but he did. A half-brother, at least. His—our—father was not averse to sowing a few wild oats of his own.'

'You mean—you mean——'

'I'm a bastard? Yes, that's right. Bastard by name, and bastard by nature, wouldn't you agree?'

'Look ...' Sara sought desperately for words to explain all this, 'I don't care who you are or why you're here. I don't even care what you think of Diane or—or the way she behaved towards your brother. What I must repeat is that—that I am not her. My—my name is Sara Fortune, as I've told you——'

'Oh, spare me the dramatics, will you?' Michael Tregower reached into his pocket and drew out a case of narrow cigars, placing one between his teeth while he sought for his lighter. 'We both know who you are and why you're here——'

'No. No, *you* don't——'

'I beg to differ.'

'Mr Tregower! Please! Listen to me!' Sara took an involuntary step forward, and as she did so his hand came out and caught her wrist, his thumb pressing cruelly against the veins on the inner side of her arm.

'No,' he denied. 'You listen to me. Adam is dead, didn't you understand what I said earlier?'

'*No!*'

'Yes.' Michael thrust his dark face closer to hers, the odour of whisky on his breath invading her nostrils. 'Dead, do you understand? By his own hand. And there was nothing I, or any of us, could do about it.'

'*No!*'

Sara moved her head futilely from side to side, her long pale hair contrasting with the darkness of her jacket, as the blood draining out of her hand had a curiously numbing effect. Staring into Michael Tregower's vengeful features she had the uncanny notion that he intended to kill her, too. That that was why he had sent for Diane, why he had threatened her in some way that forced her hand, and brought her down here. Only she hadn't come. She had sent Sara instead, hoping perhaps that the blind husband she had not seen for seven years would be unable to distinguish between them. And it might have worked, bearing in mind Sara's own instinctive compassion for the man she had thought to be Diane's husband. Whatever reason he had had for sending for his wife, she had banked on her counter-action to thwart it, though what excuse she could give Sara the girl had yet to wonder.

'I tell you, I'm not Diane Tregower!' she cried, fear forcing the note of panic into her voice. 'You've made a terrible mistake!'

'No, Diane. You made the mistake in coming here,' he declared, a mocking smile curling his lips. 'Really,

Diane, I expected better of you. Were you really disturbed by my little note? So disturbed that you made
a special journey down here—alone?'

'You—you sent for Diane?' Sara choked, trying im-
potently to free herself, but he was merciless.

'Of course,' he replied, 'Haven't I just told you?
Adam's dead. He died three weeks ago. Three weeks in
which I've thought of little else but the pleasure of
getting my hands around your selfish little neck!'

Sara's breathing had quickened alarmingly, and she
could hear her heart thundering in her ears. Her blood
pressure must be sky-high, she thought, though her
own health had never meant less to her. Even so, a
slightly hazy feeling was invading the corners of her
eyes, and although she struggled to fight the wave of
faintness that was overtaking her, the encompassing
blackness engulfed her like a welcoming shroud.

She came round to find herself lying on a dust-
sheeted sofa in a room she had not seen before. She
guessed it had been a sitting room or a drawing room,
and judging by the shapes beneath their ghostly covers,
there were other sofas and armchairs, and was that a
grand piano in the window embrasure?

The dizziness had subsided, and she was edging up
on to one elbow when Michael Tregower came into
the room carrying a glass of what looked like water.
His face was paler, too, than she remembered it, but
his eyes were just as hard when they alighted on her.
He came to stand over her as she flopped back weakly
against the cushions, and her heart began its familiar
tattoo at the flintlike coldness of his expression.

'Are you all right?' he demanded, but it was more of
an accusation than an enquiry.

'What—what happened?' she asked, playing for

time, and grim lines bracketed his mouth.

'I apparently frightened you so much, you fainted,' he declared, contemptuously, offering her the glass and when she declined, disposing of it on to the mantel-shelf, which was not shrouded. 'Or was that affected, too? If so, you're a better actress than even I gave you credit for being.'

Sara swung her legs rather shakily to the floor and sat up. His callousness almost equalled Diane's, she thought, half deciding they deserved one another. But then, remembering the murderous glint in his eyes when he had spoken of his brother's wife, she resolved not to give in to petty revenge. Nevertheless, Sara was appalled at the way Diane had sent her down here, knowing full well that she was supposed to avoid excitement of this kind.

'I think we'd better eat,' Michael Tregower said now, and Sara gazed up at him in amazement.

'Eat?'

'Why not? Mrs Penworthy's left us a cold meal in the dining room. We might as well reinforce ourselves for the night ahead.'

Sara shook her head helplessly, her eyes drawn to him in spite of her revulsion to his cruelty. How old was he? she wondered. Thirty-two, thirty-three? Was he married? Or had he avoided that state after his brother's misfortunes? Whatever, there had to have been women in his life and his remarks about the night ahead filled her with alarm. Somehow she had to re-solve this unpleasant situation before anything further happened, and getting rather unsteadily to her feet she said:

'Where's my handbag?'

'Your handbag?' Michael Tregower thrust his hands

into the waistline pockets of the moleskin pants he was wearing. Close-fitting as they were, they outlined every muscle of his powerful thighs, and she guessed with a feeling of disgust that in her place, Diane might not have found the prospect of his attention so unwelcome. 'Why do you need your handbag? You're not going anywhere.'

Sara held up her head. 'Where is my handbag?' she repeated, and after a moment's grim scrutiny of her determined features he strode impatiently out of the room.

It crossed her mind to make for the front door while he was employed in finding her bag, but as her keys were in its pocket, it seemed a futile exercise. Instead she walked rather stiffly across to the hall door and looked out.

Already he was emerging from the library again, carrying her handbag, through which he was rummaging with scant regard for her possessions.

'How—how dare you?' she gulped, as he finished his search and thrust the bag into her hands, but he merely grimaced at her.

'I wouldn't put it past you to carry a gun, sister dear,' he retorted mockingly, and she gazed open-mouthed at his effrontery. A suddenly strange expression crossed his face as he looked down at her, and almost unwillingly he reached out a hand to brush his knuckles down her cheek. She flinched away from his touch, but he was not offended, and his lips twisted with sardonic amusement. 'I must admit,' he drawled, 'Adam had better taste than I gave him credit for. No wonder he found your defection so hard to take. In his position, I might even have done the same.'

'I doubt it.' Sara found she was trembling with in-

dignation, but she couldn't help it. She had never met
a man who had treated her in this way, who held her
femininity in such low regard. Owing to her health,
and her mother's obsessive care of her, her encounters
with the opposite sex had been kept to a minimum
until Tony appeared on the scene. Her mother's death
a year ago had left her in a state of limbo, and unaware
of her weakness, Tony had come closer to her than any
man had ever been allowed to do. That was until
Diane chose to intervene, and now Sara's withdrawal
was as much an instinctive thing as an emotional one.

Michael Tregower was regarding her with guarded
eyes. 'Perhaps not,' he agreed dryly. 'No woman is
worth that kind of sacrifice. Not even you, Diane.'

Clenching her teeth, Sara scrabbled round in her
handbag and brought out her driving licence. 'There,'
she said, thrusting it at him. 'My name is Sara Fortune.
That's my licence.'

He took the plastic folder without protest, and
flicked it open. 'Sara Fortune,' he read, with dark eyebrows slightly upraised. 'Flat 3, Dolphin Court, West
Kensington. Hmm, very interesting. Who is Sara Fortune, by the way? Your secretary? Wilmer's?'

'Lance Wilmer is my father's cousin,' declared Sara
angrily. 'I tell you, I'm Sara Fortune. Why won't you
believe me?'

Michael Tregower's brows descended. 'Did you
honestly think producing a driving licence would convince me? My dear Diane, it occurs to me that if you'd
had an accident around here, it might have been hard
to explain exactly what you were doing in the area.
People in your position often travel incognito, don't
they? So—you've adopted Miss Fortune's identity, whoever she may be.'

Sara sighed. 'Haven't you ever seen Diane? Haven't you ever met her? I'm nothing like her.'

'Slim, blonde, green eyes; looks younger than her years ...' he shrugged. 'You would seem to fit the description very well. Besides,' his mouth tightened ominously, 'Adam had a picture of you in his wallet. You're Diane Tregower all right. I'd know that *inno-cent* face anywhere!'

Sara shook her head, thinking desperately. 'But don't you see?' she said at last. 'The picture Ad—your brother kept in his wallet was probably taken ten years ago. Diane's changed. She's older now. Where is the picture? Let me see it.'

'I don't have it,' he declared coldly. 'Adam would never let it out of his hands. After he was dead, it was buried with him.'

'Oh.' Sara felt as if the bottom was dropping out of her world. Then another idea came to her. 'Ring,' she said. 'Telephone London. I have Diane's number. Speak to her. See for yourself that she's really there, not here. She—she's appearing in a play at the moment.' She glanced nervously at her wrist watch. 'Ring the theatre. Surely that will convince you.'

He stared at her beneath lowering lids. 'How do I know you don't have someone waiting at the theatre, depending on this call?'

'How could I?' Sara was desperate. 'How could I know what might happen?'

He scowled. 'My note—the note you thought came from Adam was explicit enough. Come alone, it said. Tell no one where you're going.'

Sara gulped. 'Well—well, surely then, I wouldn't—have told anyone ...'

He was obviously hesitating, and she pressed a finger

on her palpitating pulse. No excitement! she thought
wryly. Dear God, she had had more excitement in the
last half hour than she had had in her whole life before. She ought to be dismayed. But she wasn't. She
had never felt the adrenalin flooding along her veins
as it was doing at the moment, and the exhilaration
that accompanied it was intoxicating.

'All right,' he said at last, when she was beginning to
give up hope of him ever agreeing to make the call.
'What's the number of the theatre? I'll speak to the
manager.'

Sara scribbled the number on a slip of paper and
handed it him. She supposed, belatedly, that she ought
to have pretended ignorance, or at least hesitated before writing down the figures. But it was too late now.
He was already crossing the hall to pick up the green
telephone that rested on the oak chest.

There was a moment's delay while he contacted the
operator at Torleven, and then Sara heard the reassuring burr of the bell ringing in the manager's office. It
seemed to ring for ages before it was answered, but
when the receiver was lifted, she found herself holding
her breath as Michael Tregower made his enquiry.

'Not there?' he said, a moment later, swinging round
to stare grimly at Sara. 'What? Taken ill? I'm sorry.
Do you know when she'll be back? Oh—I—er—I'm
just a friend. A friend of a friend, as you might say. No.
Sorry. Yes, of course. Goodbye.'

As the receiver was replaced, Sara felt her tongue
clinging to the roof of her mouth. She didn't have to be
told that Diane wasn't in the building. Even without
Michael Tregower's words, his expression said it all.

'There's panic on, apparently,' he declared without
emotion. 'Your understudy's had to take over at the

last moment, and people are demanding their money back. An unexpected illness, so your agent tells them. They don't know when you'll be able to return.'

Sara moved her head in a helpless, negative gesture. 'Diane—Diane must have planned this,' she said incredulously. 'She must have known I might try to get in touch with her ...'

'Oh, come on.' He sounded really impatient now. 'Don't you think this has gone on long enough? When you passed out just now I should have realised that no stranger was likely to react so positively. You were scared, Diane, admit it! Scared out of your tiny mind! But not half as scared as you ought to be now, knowing I know that you've burned your bridges behind you.'

Sara felt unutterably weary suddenly. It had all been too much for her. Much too much. The retort that had she known Diane would not be there, she would hardly have suggested ringing the theatre, trembled on her lips, but was never spoken. Michael Tregower would doubtless decide she had only been playing for time, for whatever defence she raised, he tore it down ruthlessly.

'I think we should eat, don't you?' he declared coldly, and with a helpless movement of her shoulders, she implied consent.

The dining room was at the back of the house, and here the blinds had been drawn to allow the last light of the evening to penetrate its shadowy corners. A lamp on a long sideboard gave illumination, and the table was laid with a white damask cloth and silver cutlery. There was a savoury quiche, a dish of cold meats, a bowl of tossed salad, and some crusty rolls. To follow there was a strawberry gateau, and Sara wished she felt more able to do justice to it. But her mind buzzed with

the possibilities of what Michael Tregower intended to
do with her—with *Diane*—and it was difficult to concentrate on anything with that nagging anxiety bringing a hectic flush to her cheeks.

'Relax,' he remarked unsympathetically, leaving her
to seat herself on one of the tapestry-covered chairs.
'For a woman of your age and apparent experience,
you're ridiculously sensitive. Or is that an act, too?
How does one tell?'

Sara subsided on to the chair at the opposite end of
the table from the one he had taken, and made no attempt to answer him. But her silence was evidently no
more acceptable than her diffidence, for he stifled a
curse as he rose again and came to take the seat at right
angles to her.

'Surely this is cosier,' he remarked with cold mockery,
and her hands tightened automatically in her lap.

She supposed she ought to tell him that as well as
being someone else, she was also suffering from a rare
heart disease that, while allowing her to lead a normal
life in ordinary circumstances could, given sufficient
stimulation, cause valvular failure and, ultimately,
death. It was a condition she had lived with all her life,
or at least as long as she could remember. Rheumatic
fever when she was scarcely out of infancy had affected
her heart, narrowing the valves and preventing them
from closing properly. Regular care and the use of
drugs had minimised the effects of the disease, but it
was always there, and in cases of extreme stress her
heart could cease to function entirely. Sara seldom
talked about it. Indeed, if anything, she was ashamed
of the weakness that her mother had guarded so vigil-
antly. After her mother's death, she had felt a sense of
freedom from the knowledge, but Tony's defection and

her subsequent withdrawal had reminded her of her
vulnerability.

Now this man, Michael Tregower, was tormenting
her, goading her, threatening her with she knew not
what. And he had no idea of the risks he was running ...

'Eat, can't you?' he said now, helping himself to a
generous slice of the savoury flan, and ladling salad on
to his plate. 'The food's good—I can vouch for it. I've
been living here for almost a week now, and Mrs Penworthy has done me proud.'

'Mrs Penworthy!'

Sara looked up with expectant eyes, and his lips
thinned. 'Oh, no,' he said irritably. 'You're not going
to tell me that the housekeeper will recognise you!
Sorry. She's only been looking after the place since
Adam went to live in Praia do Lobo. I doubt if you ever
met her.'

Sara hunched her shoulders. 'Haven't you ever seen
Diané?' she protested. 'Why, she—she's famous!'

'I'm afraid I've been living in South America for the
past fifteen years.' Did that account for his swarthy
complexion? 'Like I told you, I was always the black
sheep of the family. Old Adam, our father that is, never
wanted to see me around. I reminded him too strongly
of his ill-spent youth.'

Sara sighed. 'I see.' She paused. 'Why did—why did
Adam go to live in—where was it you said.'

'Praia do Lobo. Don't pretend you don't know. He
inherited the villa there.'

'Inherited? From whom?'

His eyes narrowed. 'All right, I'll play the game, if
you like. From Tio Jorge, of course—our father's uncle.

You knew **Adam's** grandmother was Portuguese, didn't you?'

'No.' But that explained the dark blood. 'I tell you, I only know what Diane told me.'

'Who better?' He shrugged sardonically. 'Well—our grandmother came from Coimbra. It's quite a famous town in Portugal.'

'I know of Coimbra,' retorted Sara, somewhat tartly. 'My education has not been neglected.'

'I'm glad to hear it.' His lips curled. 'So Jorge de los Santos was our grandmother's brother. His wife, Isabella, is matriarch now.'

'I understand,' Sara nodded.

'As it happens, I've been more involved with that side of the family than Adam ever was.' His eyes narrowed broodingly as he stared into the gathering dust. 'You may know that Brazil is a Portuguese-speaking country. I work there, for the Los Santos mining corporation.'

'Mining?' Sara was interested in spite of herself. 'What kind of mining?'

'Diamonds—industrial diamonds,' he added evenly. 'The Tregowers have always been involved in mining of one kind or another. You'll know about the tin mines, I'm sure.'

'Oh, yes.'

'Yes. Well, I was sent to Portugal when I was eighteen, to the university of Coimbra. For some reason my father decided that his mistakes were best kept out of the country. In any event, he did me a favour. Old Isabella likes me. She says I remind her of her late husband. It was she who sent me to Brazil.'

'I see.'

'Do you? I wonder?' His lips twisted. 'And Adam never mentioned me to you?'

'I tell you——'

'Yes, I know.' He silenced her with a look. 'So—tell me about—Sara Fortune. What does she do? Does she have a job? Or is she an actress, too?'

'Acting is working,' Sara countered, almost without thinking, and then looked down at her hands in annoyance. 'I—I work for a publishing house—the Lincoln Press. I—er—I'm an editor.'

'Really?' He forked a slice of ham on to his plate. 'An editor. How interesting!'

'It is interesting,' exclaimed Sara hotly. 'I love my work.'

'You don't have to tell me that,' he retorted thinly, and she subsided again. 'I suggest you have some food,' he added, as she continued to stare mutinously down at her hands. 'There's no point in starving yourself.'

Sara looked up. 'Why did you invite Diane down here? How did you hope to get her to agree to come?'

Michael Tregower looked at her for a long moment, then he cut a slice of the savoury flan and set it on her plate. 'Eat,' he said. 'Before I decide to starve you instead.'

Sara's clenched fists rested on the table beside her plate. 'Why won't you answer me? Don't I have a right to know?'

He continued eating for several more minutes, then he looked at her again. 'You thought Adam had sent that message, remember? You didn't even care that he had died!'

'I didn't know!'

Sara's defensive words were instinctive, but damning as well. Michael Tregower's lips curved contemptuously.

'You see,' he said. 'Play the game long enough and the victim always betrays himself.'

'Oh, you won't listen to me, will you?'

'No.'

'I—I mean me! Sara Fortune. *I* didn't know Adam was dead.'

'As Sara Fortune, why should you?'

'Why, because Diane is a friend. Because she would have told me if she knew.'

'And of course, you didn't know that Adam had been ill, seriously ill, so ill, in fact, that he wrote to you, begging you to come and see him!'

'*No!*' Sara could hardly believe it. Diane had said nothing about Adam's writing to her. On the contrary, she had led Sara to believe that he was living quite happily in Portugal, enjoying the change of scene, the warmer weather. 'When—when was this?'

'At Christmas,' replied Michael Tregower bleakly. 'Exactly three months before he died—before he took his own life!'

'No.'

'Yes.' He was implacable, and the increasing gravity of their discussion was bringing that frightening intensity back to his features. 'He had cancer, you know. It killed his mother, and it would have killed him— eventually.'

'Then——'

'Stop there!' he commanded harshly. 'I know exactly what you're going to say. But to the people who cared about him, his death was a tragedy, a terrible tragedy, that need never have happened. If you'd answered his appeal, gone to see him, shown him you were not completely heartless ...'

Sara had no answer to that but the obvious one. She was not Diane, therefore she had not known. If she had known, if Diane had confided in her, she would have urged her to go and see the man without whom she might never have been given the opportunity to meet Lance Wilmer.

Picking up her fork, she toyed with the food on her plate, her appetite dwindling completely. Then, lifting her eyes, she said: 'But—if—if Diane wouldn't come to—to see Adam in Portugal, how—how could you persuade her to come here?'

'You came,' he retorted with cold mockery, and her lids hid her anxiety.

There was a bottle of wine in an ice bucket, and now Michael Tregower reached for this, filling both their glasses with a complete disregard for Sara's protest.

'Drink it,' he said ominously. 'You may need it.'

Sara shook her head. 'What—what do you intend to do with me?' She hesitated. 'I assume you had some idea in mind.'

'Oh, yes.' His humour was sardonic. 'Although I must admit you disappoint me in some ways.'

'I—disappoint you?'

'That's right.' Darkness had fallen completely now, and his features were menacing in the lamplight. 'The woman Adam described to me was—different somehow.'

Sara held her breath. 'How different?'

He frowned. 'You're—softer. I expected a hardbitten businesswoman, but instead you appear—gentle, almost fragile. Is it an act? Was that what my brother saw in you? That gentleness, that fragility? The velvet glove that hides the iron fist?'

Sara lifted her shoulders. 'If I'm so different, why won't you believe that I'm not Diane?'

'Oh ...' he lay back in his chair, raising his glass to

his lips, 'I could be wrong. I've been wrong before. But I don't think I am. I think you're a very—astute woman, a very clever woman. But you won't fool me. Not like you fooled Adam.'

'So ...' Sara's voice quivered a little, 'we return to the point. What do you intend to do with me?'

'Well ...' He put down his glass and leaned forward, resting his arms along the table at either side of his plate. 'I'll be honest. My initial intentions bordered on the homicidal. And when I got hold of you, I—well, let's say, your timing was brilliant.'

'My—timing?'

'The faint. When you lost consciousness.' His tongue brushed his lower lip. 'Oh, yes, that was worthy of the true professional!'

Sara knew there was no point in denying that she had enforced her state of oblivion. To do so would entail explanations she was curiously loath to give. It was crazy, but there was something forbidden and exciting about what she was doing, and while she knew her mother—God rest her soul—would have been horrified by her recklessness, for the first time in her sheltered existence, she felt really alive! Not even Tony had been able to achieve that.

'You—you're saying you wanted to kill me?' she breathed, the words scarcely audible, and thick lashes veiled his eyes.

'Is that so surprising?' he demanded. 'Because of you, my brother lived a life of hell!'

'I'm sorry.'

'You're sorry!' He threw the words back at her. 'Do you think that does any good? Saying you're sorry? My God, you sit there looking the picture of innocence, with one man's death on your conscience, and the prospect of another's pending.'

Her arched brows drew together. 'I—don't understand.'

'Don't you?' he sneered. 'Why do you think I brought you down here? Not for a cosy get-together, believe me! I intended you should pay—one way or the other—for what you did to my brother.'

'One way—or the other?' she echoed.

'Yes.' He thrust himself back so that his chair tipped on to two legs. 'Death—or convicted as the murderess you are. I can't decide which affords the most satisfaction.'

Sara gasped. 'You're mad!' The sense of excitement was souring. 'I tell you, I'm not Diane.'

Michael Tregower shrugged, dropping back on to the four legs of the chair with an unnerving thud. 'No—well, there's no hurry. We've got plenty of time.'

'Plenty of time?' Sara stared at him. 'What do you mean?'

'I mean exactly what I say. We're not going anywhere. Not either of us.'

CHAPTER THREE

THE telephone was the only link with the outside world. Seated in the library, in front of a now-roaring fire, with a glass of brandy cradled between her fingers, Sara reviewed her situation. It was not particularly reassuring. Short of betraying her physical condition, Michael Tregower was unlikely to listen to her pleas, and no doubt he had already taken the phone into consideration. The front door was locked. He had not even allowed her to get her night things from the Mini. It was raining. But strangely, Sara was not afraid.

She couldn't decide about that. She couldn't decide whether her lack of fear was due to the knowledge that whatever Michael Tregower intended, it would not happen tonight—and time to delay was time to reconsider—or whether the curious sense of fatality which had gripped her since she encountered the man had made her philosophical. There was also her own reactions to him, of course. A kind of fascination—half curiosity, half revulsion, that had successfully rid her mind of all thoughts of Tony for the past few hours . . .

The door behind her opened, and she started out of her reverie. He had installed her here while he attended to other things, and although she seldom drank, she was glad of the warming fire in the brandy. As once before, a strange look crossed his face as he stared at her, then he closed the door behind him and said:

'You look quite at home. How many evenings have

you curled up in that chair with Adam for company, I wonder?'

Immediately Sara pushed her feet to the floor. It was a favourite position of hers, kicking off her shoes, and curling her legs up under her. But now she sought around for her ankle boots again, feeling too vulnerable without them.

Michael Tregower crossed the carpet swiftly and kicked them aside, causing her to look up at him indignantly.

'You won't need them tonight,' he said, and the corners of his mouth turned up slightly in a humourless smile.

Sara sighed, determining not to let him disturb her again. 'All right,' she said. 'I intended to stay here anyway. Diane's loaned me the house for a fortni——'

'The hell she has!' he snapped. 'This house is not hers to lend.'

'Hers?'

Sara couldn't resist the taunt, but it was quickly overridden. 'Yours, then,' he agreed coldly. 'You forfeited the right to Ravens Mill when you walked out on my brother.'

'Oh, yes?' Sara couldn't let that go. 'You've been out of the country too long, Mr Tregower. The law is changed. Half of everything goes to the wife at the time of a divorce or separation. And Diane and Adam were never divorced. That means——'

'You scheming little bitch!' he bit out furiously, grasping her arms and hauling her up out of the chair, so that the brandy glass spun out of her hand and splintered noisily in the grate. 'Are you daring to suggest that you own this house? That what was Adam's is now yours?'

Sara was trembling so much she could hardly stand, but his hands supported her, cruel hands that bit into the flesh of her upper arms, through the thin material of her blouse now that she had shed the jersey jacket.

'I—I was only telling you——' she stammered, as he glared down at her, and his expression changed as her colour receded.

'So pale,' he muttered. 'So fragile! No wonder you drove poor old Adam out of his mind!' and dragging her closer, he forced his mouth down on hers.

With one hand imprisoned at the nape of her neck, he held her close against him, her rounded breasts crushed against the hardness of his chest. His possession was total and suffocating, but although Sara's heart fluttered, she could feel other emotions stirring inside her. No man had ever kissed her so brutally, so adultly, so angrily—and yet, as he continued to hold her, she sensed the reluctant change that came over him.

The hand that still gripped her arm relaxed its hold, sliding across her shoulder to her neck, pushing aside the neckline of her shirt and invading the tender warmth within. She offered only a tentative resistance as his fingers caressed her bare shoulders, but when the buttons parted, she tore her mouth from his.

'No——'

'No?' he mocked, bending his head to touch her skin with his tongue. 'Hmm, you taste delicious.' His voice hardened. 'You're not wearing a bra. Did you think I didn't know?' His eyes were half closed. 'I knew. And you're beautiful ... beautiful ...'

His hand cupped one rose-tipped breast as he spoke, massaging its swollen fullness with caressing appreciation, exploring the hardening nipple with disturbing effect.

'You—you shouldn't,' she protested, but the hands she raised to stop him only clung to him, and as if he sensed her weakness, his gentleness fled.

With a rough gesture he dragged the shirt across her breasts and turned away from her, saying violently: 'I swore on my brother's grave that I would make you pay for what you'd done to him! God, how was I to know you'd *enjoy* it?'

His words were hurting and humiliating, as he had intended them to be, and Sara's fingers shook as she fastened the buttons of her shirt. She felt ashamed. What was the matter with her? she asked herself disgustedly. This man had already threatened to take her life, and she was permitting him intimacies she had never permitted any man before. Tony had tried to pet with her, but she had always maintained a certain detachment before, something she had put down to the uncertainty of her condition. Now, she realised, she was no different from any other woman. She *had* wanted Michael Tregower to touch her, she had wanted to touch *him*! He was right: she had enjoyed it.

He turned back to her then, his hands thrust deep into the pockets of his pants as if afraid he might be tempted to touch her once more. 'Go to bed!' he ordered curtly! 'Get out of my sight! I need to think.'

Sara's mouth was dry. 'Bed?' she echoed. 'You really expect me to go to bed?'

'Why not?' He was contemptuous. 'You have nothing to fear from me!'

Sara glanced towards the door. 'But where do I sleep?'

'How about the room you shared with Adam? That should prove unpleasant enough. Just think of the memories it will invoke.'

Sara held up her head. 'At—at the risk of being a bore, I must repeat that as I am not Diane, I have no idea which room she shared with your brother.'

His mouth tightened. 'You really are a bitch, aren't you?'

'No!' Sara was indignant. 'Mr Tregower——'

'Oh, shut up, will you?' He glared furiously at her. 'Just get out of here, can't you? Before I do something I, for one, will regret.'

Sara pressed her lips together. 'Mr Tregower——'

'Oh, for God's sake!' With an oath, he crossed the room, swung open the door and strode towards the stairs. 'Follow me,' he directed angrily, and albeit hesitantly she did so.

The portrait at the first landing mocked her. It had to be Michael's father, or his grandfather, but the likeness was unmistakable. Indeed, judging by that elder Tregower's dour expression, Michael was more like his ancestors than Adam had ever been. This man, like Michael, would never let a woman make a fool of him, and she guessed Adam's mother must have been responsible for the weaker side of his nature.

Noticing her hesitation before the portrait, Michael paused and said contemptuously: 'Yes, old Adam's still here. What's the matter? Afraid he might come and exact his own revenge?'

Sara shuddered. 'No.' But she looked over her shoulder as she followed Michael along the landing. 'Who—who is he? Adam's grandfather?'

He halted before double panelled doors, and looked at her with scornful eyes. 'As if you didn't know,' he retorted. 'Do you know why he went to Portugal to choose a wife? Because he found the English women too forward—they had too much to say for themselves.

Can you imagine what he would have thought of someone like you?'

Sara chose not to answer, and Michael swung open
the doors into what was obviously the master bedroom
of the house. A switch brought several lamps into warm
illumination, and she saw a room of generous proportions, squarely dominated by a large fourposter bed.
The walls were hung with cream silk damask, which
matched the covers on the bed; the furniture was dark
wood, oak or mahogany, tallboys vying with the triple-
mirrored dressing table for space. There were two
striped Regency chairs, a matching chaise-longue, and
an antique writing desk stood in the window embrasure. The room had been clearly used, there were
no dust-sheets here, and various articles of male usage
were draped over the backs of the chairs or set upon the
dressing table.

'This—this is your room,' said Sara faintly, as he
gestured her inside. 'I can't use your room.'

Michael made a sound of disgust. 'You'll have to. It's
the only bed that's made up, and if sleeping between
my sheets is distasteful to you, I should tell you Mrs
Penworthy changed them this morning.'

Sara gulped. 'Where—where will you sleep?'

'You care!' he sneered. 'Well, not here, at any rate.
You can face your ghosts alone.'

Sara made a helpless movement of her hands. 'Mr
Tregower——'

'Go to sleep!' he retorted, and strode out of the
room.

The door slammed dully behind him, and she heard
his footsteps receding along the landing. Only then
did she realise exactly how tautly she had been holding

herself, and her shoulders sagged beneath a weight of unexpected depression.

It had been an incredible evening, but now that it was over the anti-climactic feeling of dejection was crippling. For the past few hours she had been living on a high stimulus that was all the more debilitating to someone who had never experienced it before. Fencing with Michael Tregower had been an intoxicating game that left her feeling drained and weary.

Looking round the room again, she remembered with a pang that she had left her handbag downstairs. The bottle with the tablets she was supposed to take was inside it, and the prospect of going downstairs again and braving Michael's anger and his cynicism was more than she could anticipate. She would just have to wait until he was in bed—however long that might be.

The bathroom adjoining the bedroom was just as luxurious. Cream tiles, inset with yellow roses, chrome-plated taps, and a metal shower compartment. There were fluffy yellow towels, and a dark blue bathrobe hung behind the door, a suitable garment to wear after she had shed her clothes.

She took a shower, keeping her hair dry as best she could, and then after towelling herself dry and using some of the rather masculine-flavoured talc she found in the glass cabinet which hung above the hand basin, she shrugged into the bathrobe.

It was huge, obviously masculine too, and she hesitated a moment, wondering whether it might have belonged to Adam. But no. The tang of shaving soap about it, and a faint odour she didn't recognise, but which she guessed rather nervously was the sweat from Michael's body, convinced her it had been in use recently. It was a disturbing thought, and she stood in front of the long wardrobe mirror when she returned to the bedroom, viewing her appearance with faint embarrassment.

Her hair, the straight hair she had given up trying to curl, hung loosely about her shoulders, though the enveloping folds of the bathrobe disguised the slenderness of her body. The robe almost reached her ankles, for she was not much above medium height whereas Michael Tregower was easily six feet. She tightened the cord about her slim waist as the neckline threatened to open, and curled her toes into the cream and green pile of the carpet. If her friends could see her now, she thought wryly, and then frowned as she remembered Diane.

Where was she? That was the all-important question. How could she do this to the girl she had always pretended affection for? Diane had few girl friends, her overwhelming ambition and supreme self-confidence left little room for emotional attachments of that kind, but Sara would never have believed she could treat *her* so callously. Diane, of all people, knew of her vulnerability. Yet, without any warning, she had catapulted her into a situation she must know was unpredictable.

Sara shook her head. Of course, Diane did not know that Adam was dead, but because of whatever Michael's note had said, she had needed a scapegoat. Had she been upset by it? Or had she assumed that Sara would be able to handle a blind man? Whatever, she had absented herself from the theatre, and left Sara to cope as best she might. That was unforgivable.

With a sigh, Sara picked up a man's hairbrush from the dressing table and began to stroke it through her hair. Tomorrow, she thought, pulling a face at herself,

tomorrow she would have to tell Michael Tregower all
about herself. It had been exciting, pretending to be
normal again, but it could not go on. She would not
allow it to go on. Never again would she let any man
treat her as Tony had treated her. Tomorrow she
would show Michael the medication she had been prescribed, and suffer the change that would come over
him ...

Putting down the brush again, she padded over to
the bed. The sheets were silk, she saw uneasily, soft and
smooth and undoubtedly expensive. The pillowcases
were lace-edged, to match the heavy coverlet, itself
exquisitely embroidered in silk damask.

Toying with the cord of the bathrobe, she seated herself on the side of the bed. For the first time she became
aware of the distant thunder of the ocean, and of the
uncanny silence around the house. Had Michael Tregower retired already? She sighed. Her flat in London
was within constant sight and sound of traffic and
people, and the remoteness of Ravens Mill would have
been unnerving at any time. With the events of the
evening still firmly fixed in her mind, it was doubly so,
and the wind sifting under the door did little to restore
her confidence.

Was this the room Diane had shared with Adam? It
had to be. It was such a big bedroom, and even illumin-
ated with half a dozen lamps, there were still shadows
in dark corners.

She smoothed her fingers over the pillows. What had
Michael meant about his grandfather coming to exact
revenge? Was the house haunted? Diane had never
mentioned it, but then would she? She hadn't mentioned that it was a huge mausoleum, had she?

She sighed, and padded across the room again to

extinguish four of the lamps, leaving only the two beside the bed still lighted. She refused to plunge the room into total darkness, for total darkness it would be in this isolated spot.

Standing beside the bed again, she looked down at the bathrobe. She wasn't cold, and she had no intention of dressing again before going downstairs. The shower and her over-imagination were acting like a fever on her blood, and she could have descended the stairs naked without feeling chilled.

Sitting on the edge of the huge bed, she drew up her knees and wrapped her arms around them. It was remarkable really, she thought. She had left London that morning for a couple of weeks' escape from the problems of her life. And now here she was, facing reality in all its harsh perspective.

She became aware of a niggling pain in her chest. It was not severe. It might be indigestion, caused by the extreme tension she had experienced that evening, but it reminded her of the tablets in her handbag downstairs, and of her intention to go and get them. The house seemed quiet enough, in all conscience. Michael Tregower must have gone to bed.

The door seemed to make an awful noise opening, but she realised it was her heightened senses that accentuated its natural usage. Hastening along the landing, she descended the stairs without hesitation, finding the open library door without too much difficulty in the faint illumination from the dying fire.

Her handbag was lying by the chair where she had left it, and opening it quickly, she extracted the bottle containing the tablets. Then, going across to the tray of drinks, she poured herself some tonic water and swallowed the medication eagerly. She swayed as she replaced the bottle in her handbag, and then, not wanting to arouse suspicion, she replaced it by the chair where she had found it.

She was coming out of the library again when the lights were switched on, and looking up she saw Michael standing at the fork of the stairs. It was too much for her, encountering him again like that, and she grasped the bannister wearily, hardly able to put one foot in front of the other.

With an oath, he came down the stairs towards her, and before she could protest, he swung her into his arms and carried her back up to the first floor.

'Wh-what are you doing?' she stammered, endeavouring to regain her composure, aware of the strength of the arms about her, and his expression mirrored his sarcasm.

'I was about to ask you the same question,' he declared. 'I heard a—noise. I thought I ought to make sure it wasn't old Adam come to haunt you.'

Sara swallowed. 'You—you didn't think that at all!' she denied hotly, as he strode along the corridor to her room. 'You probably saw me go downstairs, and decided to frighten me.'

Michael regarded her mockingly. 'You've made yourself at home, at any rate,' he remarked, entering her bedroom and setting her down beside the bed. 'Is this for my benefit?'

Sara flushed then, a becoming rose colour that spread up from the neckline of the bathrobe to the roots of her pale hair. 'If—if you mean this ...' she indicated the robe, 'it—it was the only thing I could use.'

'I'm not objecting, am I?' he enquired. 'And I imagine you can justify your reasons for creeping about my house.'

'I wasn't—creeping about.' Sara held up her head. 'I—I needed some—aspirin.'

'The age-old remedy. How prosaic! Can't you do better than that, Diane? The doors are all locked, and I have the keys.'

She gasped. 'You can't honestly imagine I'd try to escape in a bathrobe!'

His eyes narrowed. 'How shall I answer that? Do I take it you've decided you like it here?'

'Take it any way you like.' She stared at him angrily. 'Now if you don't mind, I'd like to go to sleep.'

'I don't mind,' he averred, stepping aside and indicating the bed with a mocking hand. 'I—er—I'll just take my bathrobe, if I may.'

Her lips parted in dismay. 'You—you wouldn't!'

'Why not? It's mine, isn't it?' His lids flickered. 'Of course, if you don't want to *give* it to me ...'

Realising his meaning, Sara's fingers fumbled over the knot. If he suspected that she didn't want to give it to him, he would take it. Unloosening the cord, she turned her back on him, dropping the robe to the floor as she scrambled rather inelegantly between the sheets.

'Thank you.' He bent and picked up the robe, but he did not move away from the bed, and she held the covers determinedly under her chin, aware of that disruptive excitement taking hold of her again. 'I'll say goodnight, then.'

She nodded, hardly daring to speak. 'Goodnight,' she got out chokily, and his eyes revealed his curiosity.

'Lost your nerve?' he enquired coldly, resting one hand on the post at the head of the bed. 'You seem ... nervous. Have I old Adam to thank for this?'

Sara closed her eyes, hoping against hope he would just go, but he didn't. The depression of the springs revealed that he had dropped down on to the bed beside her, and was obviously waiting for her to make the next move.

She tried to think coherently. What had happened between them downstairs returned in a wave of heat across her body, but she remembered, too, the way he had reacted. So long as he thought she was willing, he would not touch her. It was only if he thought she was afraid of him that he might change his mind about her.

Opening her eyes again, she looked up into his face, and was surprised at the torment she found there. Realising he must be thinking of his brother, she propped herself up on her elbows, holding the sheet in place with one hand and touching his face with the other. He flinched away from her fingers, but he didn't get up, and stiffening her resolve, she said: 'Were you really concerned about me, Michael?' in a soft voice.

His jaw hardened then. The contempt he felt for her was eloquent in every line of his bitter mouth, but still he lingered. 'So innocent,' he muttered, half to himself. Then: 'Aren't you afraid I might decide to share the bed with you?'

'I can't stop you,' she replied honestly, although she was amazed he could not hear the thunderous beating of her heart.

'No, you can't,' he agreed through thin lips, but his narrowed eyes revealed a smouldering passion she had not seen before.

Almost against his will it seemed, he leant over her, forcing her to drop her elbows and fall back against the pillows. With her breath whistling with laboured efforts through her lungs, he touched her lips with his fingers, caressing them, parting them, his eyes never leaving the startled dilation of hers.

'Not so provocative now, are we?' he taunted

thickly, bending his head to stroke her lips with his tongue. 'You're panicking, Diane—I can feel it. Your heart's fluttering like a trapped bird, and that's exactly what you are, Diane. A trapped bird in the claws of a hawk. And nothing you say can save you now.'

'You—you're mad——' she choked, but his lips against the skin of her shoulder were frankly disturbing, and she knew she was weakening.

She lifted her hands protestingly, but they slid harmlessly over the smooth silk of his shirt, and he laughed low in his throat. 'That's right,' he applauded mockingly. 'Try to stop me. Then we'll see who wins the battle.'

Sara turned her head from side to side on the pillows, seeking some means of escape, aware that her own body was betraying her with every movement it made. He had unbuttoned his shirt and the abrasive skin of his chest made her breasts tingle pleasurably, and her blood ran like fire along her veins.

But, unwillingly, she was arousing him, too. The eyes that despised her were glazing, and there was a certain roughness in his touch that spoke of emotions getting out of control.

'You—you bitch——' he muttered, as if the words would work some miracle of revulsion against her. But he was on the bed beside her, his legs kicking the covers aside, the weight of his body imprisoning her beneath him. His lips took the place of his fingers, and her head sank into the pillows beneath the possessive demand of his mouth.

Her hands sought his shoulders of their own volition, stretching and expanding against his smooth flesh with sensual enjoyment. She couldn't deny the purely physical pleasure of feeling his taut muscles beneath

her fingers, the strong corded muscles that ran down
his back to his thighs. She could feel every muscle and
her own betraying response, and with that awareness
she lost her last hold on reality. She didn't care if he
thought she was Diane, she realised recklessly. He smelt
so warm and male, his limbs enveloping her completely, seeking a possession she had no will to resist.
She let the demands of her body dictate her reason,
urging him to go on, holding her, caressing her, kissing her, giving her whatever it was he had to give.

Then, just when she was beginning to believe, half
in anticipation, half in fear, that he did indeed intend
to make love to her, a shudder of revulsion ran through
his body, and he dragged himself back from the preci-
pice. He was trembling. She could feel the tormented
muscles of his thighs protesting his withdrawal, but
with a forceful effort he hauled himself up from the
bed.

'Oh, yes,' he muttered, thrusting his shirt back into
his pants with unsteady fingers, 'yes, you'd like me to
lose control, wouldn't you, Diane? What a triumph
that would be, knowing you could seduce me as well
as my brother!'

'You're mad!'

It was Sara who protested now, thrusting herself up
on her elbows, uncaring at this moment how provocative she seemed. Was he so insensitive to her feelings?
She was not so insensitive to his. Whatever he said
now, however he reacted, the man who had just kissed
her and caressed her had done so with feeling, not with
cold hostility, and his withdrawal had been as painful
to him as it was to her.

'I'm not mad, Diane,' he said now, turning away.
'You'll find out how sane I am in the morning. Dif-

ferent situations demand different measures, that's all.
You're cleverer than I gave you credit for being. Which
just shows you should never underestimate an adver-
sary!'

The door slamming behind him was as chilling as
the draught it caused across her body. Looking down at
her firm breasts, full and swollen with the emotions he
had aroused in her, she felt a renewed sense of disbelief.
Was this really happening to her? Was she really lying
here in a strange bed, as naked as the day she was born,
actually feeling a sense of regret because a man who
had been a stranger to her until a few hours ago had
refused to sleep with her?

He was right. He wasn't mad, *she was*. He had done
nothing to be ashamed of. He truly believed she was
Diane, and she had allowed him to go on thinking so.

With a feeling of disgust she pulled the sheets
around her, hiding her nakedness from her own eyes.
Was she so disreputable? she wondered anxiously. Had
she really no justification for her actions? Would anyone—*would he*?—understand her motives when they
were revealed? Maybe in the morning, she thought,
sinking back against the pillows, maybe then she could
explain ... But would he ever forgive her?

CHAPTER FOUR

It was broad daylight when Sara awakened. The sun was pouring through the cracks in the blinds, and a sleepy examination of her watch face solicited the knowledge that it was already after ten.

'Ten!'

She said the word out loud, and as she did so, the memory of the events of the previous night came back in sharp focus. That terrible scene when she had practically thrown herself at him haunted her, and she pressed agonised fingers to her lips as she recalled her abandoned behaviour. Then, with a sigh, she shook her head. She should not feel embarrassment for something he had instigated. Whatever her reactions, he had *wanted* her. She was convinced of that.

Her body, which had stiffened, now yielded again upon the mattress, and she closed her eyes against the harsh light of day that cast such a different reflection on her behaviour. It was impossible not to consider what kind of girl he might think her when he found out she was not Diane. After living in South America for so many years, his attitudes were bound to be different.

It had been so unlike her. She, who was normally so controlled, so detached, so very much in command of every situation. She had never encouraged intimate relationships, even her association with Tony had been governed more by an intellectual rather than a physical compatibility. She had never seen herself as a sexual person, and consequently she had avoided involvements of that kind.

Yet suddenly all that was changed. Last night Michael Tregower had awakened her to an awareness of her own femininity, and in so doing had aroused emotions she had never known she possessed. And, like a child, she had turned to him, responded to him, allowed him to get closer to her, both physically and mentally, than any man had ever done before.

A wave of colour stained her cheeks. How could she face him again, after what had happened? How could she see him, talk with him, act naturally with him when only hours before she had behaved like a wanton in his arms? What had happened to her constraint, her inhibitions, her self-respect?

The opening of the bedroom door caused her to close her eyes tightly once more, feigning sleep, but it was apparently useless. The smell of coffee was an aromatic temptation, and half opening one eye, she found Michael standing watching her with wry speculation.

'Stop pretending,' he ordered curtly, setting the tray down on the table beside her. 'It would be foolish to antagonise me so early in the morning, and as we've been almost as intimate as two people can be, it would seem a foolish notion, don't you think?'

Sara blinked, and compressed her lips, noticing with some relief that he was dressed. 'I—I've just woken up,' she said defensively. 'How—how long have you been up?'

'Not long,' he assured her, going to the windows to open the blinds. 'It's a glorious morning. I couldn't wait to continue our stimulating friendship.'

'I see.' Sara gulped. 'You mean your relationship with Diane, of course.'

'God!' Michael ran a hand round the back of his neck, flexing his shoulder muscles. 'I felt sure you would have seen the futility of that argument by now, Diane. Don't you think it's time we stopped playing games, and acted like two responsible people?'

Sara levered herself up on the pillows, making sure to keep the silken covers closely about her. There was toast and coffee on the tray, as well as a glass of freshly-squeezed orange juice, and she drank this before attempting to answer him.

'Did Mrs Penworthy prepare this?' she asked, risking his anger, and he interrupted his frowning contemplation of the view to turn back to her.

'No, I did,' he retorted harshly, thrusting his hands into the pockets of his pants. 'I'm not entirely useless. I can make coffee and boil an egg. And wash up, too, if I have to. Of course, now you're here, I shall expect you to tackle that task.'

Sara sighed. 'About—what you said earlier.' She paused as he stiffened. 'I agree. I think we should stop playing games. I'm not Diane, and there's no way you're going to make me say I am. And if you'll give me long enough to get dressed, I'll prove it to you.'

'How?' He was sceptical.

Sara licked her lips. *By going downstairs this minute and showing you the tablets I've got in my bag!* an inner voice screamed silently, but her tongue clove to the roof of her mouth, and she couldn't say the words.

'You see!' He didn't wait for her hesitant response. 'As soon as I challenge you, you're sunk. You're playing for time, Diane, and I'm in no hurry to bait my trap. If it were not for Adam, I could almost enjoy tormenting you!'

'If it were not for Adam, you wouldn't be here!' she retorted tremulously, and he inclined his head.

'True.' He regarded her mockingly for a few moments, and then, as her lips parted beneath his intent gaze, his eyes hardened. 'So innocent!' he muttered, half to himself. 'So feminine.' His mouth twisted. 'I could almost say you're the first woman I've seen who looks good in the morning, which shows how deceptive appearances can be.'

Sara held up her head. 'I suppose you've seen lots of women in the mornings.'

'Some,' he agreed dryly. 'You wouldn't expect me to lie, would you?'

'I don't particularly care what you do,' Sara replied tautly, 'so long as you let me go.'

'Which you know I won't do.'

Sara drew a deep breath. 'Why? Because you want me?' she demanded, deliberately taunting him. He wasn't the only one who could enjoy the fleeting feeling of power it gave, but his response was much different from hers.

With a cruel smile he came to the bed and cupped her chin in his hand, turning her face up to his with insistent strength. 'Don't push your luck, Diane,' he intoned huskily, while his free hand roamed familiarly beneath the tightly-clutched sheet, finding the hardened point of her breast. 'If I thought——'

He broke off abruptly and set her free, and she fell back against the pillows, the pounding of her heartbeats filling her ears. His instinctive reaction had shown her just how vulnerable she still was, and how foolish it could be to prolong this masquerade.

'So,' he said, in control again. 'Get dressed. I'm an impatient man, remember that, and if you're not downstairs in'—he consulted his wrist watch—'fifteen minutes, I'll come and fetch you myself.'

'With a whip, no doubt,' declared Sara, refusing to

be intimidated, and his expression grew tormenting once more.

'What a splendid idea,' he mocked, surveying her critically. 'Perhaps I will at that. So be sure you're not in the bathroom when I arrive. I understand wet leather has the sting of a knife blade.'

With a polite bow he left her, and Sara lay for several minutes after he had gone, wondering whether he really could be that cruel. Somehow, in spite of everything, she doubted it. She didn't know what it was, he had certainly given her no reason to trust him, and yet she sensed he was not entirely ruthless. It was something she felt, something she knew in her bones; a belief compounded of the reluctant compassion he had exhibited when she fainted, and the instinctive response her body had felt towards the mastery of his. No man without mercy would have treated her to such a display of passion or encouraged the kind of response she had been so eager to give.

Even so, she did not trust him not to come back if she disobeyed him, and gulping down a cup of coffee, she hastened into the bathroom. Her clothes were where she had left them, and she dressed quickly, and without interruption. Then, after subjecting her hair to a vigorous brushing, she made her way downstairs.

There were sounds emanating from the back of the house, and following their lead, she came to the kitchen. She had expected to find Michael washing up, despite his protestations to the contrary, and after steeling herself for the encounter she was almost disappointed to find a strange woman working efficiently at the sink, lifting washed plates on to a stainless steel drainer.

'Oh ...' Sara's instinctive reaction was overheard,

and the woman turned sharply, her homely features adopting a curious smile when she saw the girl.

'Ah, you must be Miss Fortune,' she said, and Sara was shocked to hear her name on the woman's lips. But obviously Michael had considered it simpler to avoid unnecessary explanations. 'Mr Tregower said you'd slept late. You're here for a holiday, I gather. I'm sorry I didn't know you were coming, or I'd have had beds prepared.'

'That's all right.' Sara couldn't prevent the wave of colour that swept up her cheeks as she considered what the woman must be thinking. She glanced round awkwardly. 'Er—where is Mr Tregower? I was—looking for him.'

'He's outside, I fancy. He said something about not unpacking your car last night because of the rain. No doubt he's doing that now.'

'Oh! Oh, thank you.' Sara could feel the colour draining out of her cheeks again. Why hadn't she thought of that? Michael would obviously unpack the car. And what would he make of its contents? She hardly felt prepared to contemplate.

Leaving the kitchen, she hurried back into the hall. Sure enough, her suitcases were standing in the middle of the floor, but there was no sign of Michael. However the front door stood open, and responding to the rush of air, which was not as chilly now as it had been the evening before, she walked to the entrance. The scent of the sea was unmistakable, and she breathed deeply, loving the clean fresh fragrance of the ocean after the pollution of the city, and then started back in alarm when her host appeared from behind the Mini. He saw her as he straightened from doing something inside the vehicle, and as he came towards her she saw the puzzled anger in the intensity of his gaze.

'Tell me something,' he said, as he reached her, supporting himself with one hand on either side of the
doorway, so that she fell back another step. 'Why
would Diane fetch down a sleeping bag and a box of
groceries, when she had no intention of spending the
night here?'

Sara took a deep breath. 'If—if you think about that,
I—I think you'll come up with—with an answer,' she
said unevenly. 'And—and it's very kind of you to unpack for me, but—but totally unnecessary. I—I shan't
be staying.'

'Won't you?' The words were heavy and loaded with
meaning. Then, more impatiently, he added: 'Who
the hell is Sara Fortune?'

'You—you know,' she protested, taking another
backward step, and he released his supporting hold on
the door to follow her.

'I think you'd better come into the library,' he said,
and with a helpless shrug she complied, no more eager
than he was to have their confrontation overheard.

The library was chilly. The remains of the previous
night's fire had not been removed, and Sara thought
fatalistically that they epitomised the destruction of
her own brief spell of excitement. Michael closed the
door, and then, folding his arms, he said harshly:

'Did Diane send you here? Because I warn you——'

Sara twisted her hands together. 'Diane—Diane did
send me here, but'—quickly, as his expression hardened,—'only—only in a manner of speaking.'

'What the hell's that supposed to mean?'

'Let me explain.' Pulling her lower lip between her
teeth, she sought for words. 'I—I wanted to get away
from London for a while.'

'How convenient!'

'No, I mean it. I—Diane offered me this place.'

'Offered it to you?'

'To stay. To get away.'

'At exactly this time?' He sounded sceptical.

'Well, yes, as it happens. Of course, she didn't tell me the—the house was occupied.

'*Occupied!*' The word was a harsh denigration of himself. 'My God! Do you realise what she almost did? What *I* almost did?'

Sara's cheeks suffused with colour. 'I should.'

He paced aggressively across the floor and then turned to face her. 'So? If I'm to believe you, you're completely innocent of any of Diane's tricks?'

Sara shrugged. 'I didn't know you were here, if that's what you mean. If you believe that.'

'Is it the truth?'

'Yes!' Sara gasped indignantly.

'All right, I do believe you.'

'You do?' Sara realised it sounded bad, but after the past few hours she could hardly believe it was over. *And without her revealing the truth about herself.*

Michael studied her anxious expression for a few moments longer and then nodded. 'I should have guessed, I suppose,' he muttered, raking angry fingers through his hair. 'That—innocence! It was too real to be faked. I must have scared the hell out of you!'

Sara quivered. 'Not—not altogether.'

He shook his head. 'But God! Why didn't you stop me?'

'How?'

He shrugged. 'That car out there is a moving vehicle of your identity. Sleeping bag, groceries, a manuscript!

Not to mention a pair of walking shoes Diane would probably be found dead before wearing!'

Sara hesitated. 'You might have said it was all deliberate.'

'Food? Diane? No, I don't think so.' Then he sighed. 'Oh, I don't know. Maybe you're right. Maybe last night I was a little—mad! Crazy! Not least'—he paused—'because I didn't honestly want to believe it was true!'

Now Sara's palms grew moist. 'I—I don't know what you mean.'

'Oh, come on.' Michael halted in front of her. 'You're not that naïve. You proved it just now—upstairs. You knew when I was—touching you last night that there was more to my actions than a lust for revenge. I liked touching you, Sara Fortune. And in spite of everything, you liked me touching you, too.'

Sara stepped back. 'I—think this conversation has gone far enough,' she murmured a little chokily. Clearing her throat, she added: 'As—as the matter seems to have been cleared up to your satisfaction——'

'Like hell it has!' he interrupted her angrily, and she blinked at him. 'I want to know more about why Diane sent you here, how she achieved it. From what I've heard of my sister-in-law, it just can't be a coincidence.'

Sara lifted her shoulders. 'I told you, I—I needed a break.'

'But why did you need a break? And why this week? Surely Cornwall in April is not everyone's idea of paradise?'

Sara frowned. Then, squaring her shoulders, she said: 'There was—a man——'

'A man?' He frowned. 'What man?'

'A man I knew,' she explained defensively. 'I—oh, I thought he cared about me——'

'—and he didn't?'

'Apparently not.' She shrugged awkwardly. 'He—well, we stopped seeing one another.'

'And I suppose Diane had nothing to do with that?'

'Diane?' Sara looked up at him, and then her eyes clouded doubtfully. 'I—well, only indirectly.'

'Go on!'

Sara swallowed. 'I'd rather not.'

'*Sara!*'

It was the first time he had used her own name, and on his lips it was a very attractive sound.

'There was something,' she confessed. 'Something Diane—told him. At the time, it seemed coincidental, but now——'

'Now you don't think so?'

'I don't know what to think.'

'That makes two of us,' he growled, pushing back his hair with angry fingers. 'God, when I think of what might have happened! You may regard me as some kind of stud, but believe me, I'm not in the habit of—of seducing young women!'

'You didn't.'

'No, but I might have done,' he snapped shortly. Then more angrily: 'I'm sorry. Perhaps you're disappointed!'

Sara gasped. 'I——'

'Oh, all right, all right.' He sounded driven. 'I'm sorry. I'm taking it out on you, and it's not your fault. But good lord, what kind of woman is Diane to send you in her place!'

'Well,' said Sara, trying to be reasonable, 'it doesn't really matter now, does it? I—I mean, it's over.'

'Is it?'

'What do you mean?'

'I mean—oh, hell! I don't know. I need to think about this.'

'You'll have plenty of time, after I've gone.'

'Gone?' His brows drew together. 'You're not leaving?'

'I must.'

'Why?'

'Why?' Sara spread her hands helplessly. 'I can't stay here now. Not—not now.'

'Why must you leave?'

Sara could not sustain his disturbing appraisal. 'I—haven't you got things to do?' she ventured. 'Diane——'

'To hell with Diane!' he declared heavily. 'I don't care if I never see her.' He made an impatient gesture. 'She must be more astute than I imagined. Right now, all I feel towards her is disgust. Vengeance seems curiously void. You are my concern, not Diane. And I—want you to stay.'

'I—can't.'

'Why can't you?' He was brusque again. 'You said yourself, you'd planned to spend two weeks here. Why don't you do that? I promise I won't—make a nuisance of myself. And I think you know—you have nothing to fear from me.'

Sara's cheeks burned. 'You don't understand,' she began with difficulty, realising her opportunity to be completely honest had come. 'I—there are things you—you don't know about me . . .'

Michael's surveillance was mocking now. 'I think I know most of what there is to know,' he remarked dryly, and then gave in to a curiously tender impulse to stroke her cheek. 'You're too innocent to have any great secret. Tell me what it is, then I can decide whether I'm in any moral danger by allowing you to stay.'

He was not taking her seriously, and her desire to confess fled. Why should she tell him, after all? she argued with herself. They were virtually strangers, in spite of the intimacies they had shared. Once she left Ravens Mill she would never see him again. This realisation roused a curious ache in her chest, and this time she sensed there was no physical cause, which was no more reassuring.

Yet, if she stayed here, how could she hope to keep her illness from him? Sooner or later he was bound to discover her taking tablets, or maybe even find the tablets themselves. He was an intelligent man. He probably knew the name of the drug she used, and the reasons why it was prescribed. She dreaded his reactions if he ever found out for himself.

'Are you afraid to stay here?' Michael's expression had hardened now, and he was regarding her with faint contempt. 'I've told you, I won't bother you—unless you want me to.'

Sara quivered. 'It—it's an impossible situation.'

'Why is it?'

She shook her head, a feeling of apprehension sweeping over her. She could not explain without betraying herself, and she cast about helplessly for an alternative excuse.

'I—I had intended to work,' she declared. 'I—I thought the house was empty. I—needed time alone to —to work on—on my writing.'

'Your writing?' Michael frowned. 'You mean the manuscript I found?'

Sara hesitated, but then realised she would have to tell him the truth. 'It's—a novel,' she replied. 'For children. I'd planned to—to rewrite it, to shorten it a little.'

Michael shook his head. 'Well, well. An authoress, no less!'

'I'd prefer it if you said—writer,' she amended, and his lips twisted.

'Women's Lib?' he queried. 'Ms Fortune.'

'I'm sure it amuses you,' she retorted stiffly. 'But I take my work seriously.'

'Oh, I believe it.' Michael regarded her between narrowed lids. 'So—Ravens Mill was to be your—retreat?'

Sara held up her head. 'In a manner of speaking.'

'I see.' He paused, supporting himself with one hand along the mantelpiece beside her. 'And my presence—would be a distraction?'

Sara looked into his mocking eyes for a long disturbing minute, then turned and walked back into the hall. She checked her suitcases, giving them her undivided attention when there was no need to do so, and then turned schooled features towards him.

'I—I won't thank you for your hospitality. Mr Tregow——'

'*Mr Tregower!*' he snapped irritably. Then he tugged impatiently at the hair growing at the back of his neck. 'Oh, Sara! Can't we stop that stupid charade? You know you're not going anywhere. I can't—I *won't* let you. Not yet, at any rate.' His eyes swung restlessly round the hall. 'We need time to talk. For God's sake, can't you see?' His gaze riveted hers now. 'We can't just—go our separate ways! I don't want to.' He sighed exasperatedly. 'Please, try and understand what I'm saying. Sara, I want you to stay.'

She trembled, and immediately he covered the space between them, taking her cold hands between both of his, warming them by the pressure.

'Don't look at me like that,' he muttered. 'I know I haven't done anything thus far to warrant your liking or respect, but believe me, I do have feelings, and right now I could flay myself for the way I've treated you.'

'There's no need——'

'Damn you, let me decide what need there is.' He looked down at her trapped hands, and she quivered at the intimacy he could imbue into that small gesture. 'If you'll stay, at least I can pretend you—like me a little.'

Sara struggled to free herself. 'And—and what do you intend to do?' she demanded. 'Stay here too? I thought you told me your work was in—in Brazil. When do you plan to go back there? How can you afford to waste so much time in England?'

A flicker of emotion crossed his face at her accusing words, and then he said quietly: 'Since Adam is dead, Isabella wants me to remain in Portugal. And for the present I have Adam's affairs to clear up.'

'Well, surely that means—seeing Diane?'

'Not necessarily. The Tregower solicitors can deal with all that. If, as you say, Diane is entitled to half her late husband's estate, then that will have to be—considered.' He paused. 'But that has nothing to do with us—with *you*.' His eyes seemed to look right through her, dark and penetrating, and disturbingly intent. 'Stay—I'll keep out of your way, I promise. I may even have to go up to London for a few days. During the day, you could pretend I wasn't here. The house is big enough, in all conscience. Give us time to get to know one another properly.'

'You don't want to get to know me.' Sara didn't know

why she said it, but she had to have their relationship
clear between them. 'You expected Diane, and—and I
turned up. You don't owe me anything . . .'

'Sara!' His fingers hurt hers now. 'What is the matter with you? Why should you imagine I don't want to
know you? Sara . . . little Sara . . .' He raised her fingers
to his lips and her heart began its erratic tattoo. 'You
couldn't be more wrong. I find you utterly—enchant-
ing. You're the most attractive woman I've ever met,
and I don't just mean physically—although you're that
too.' His lips twitched. 'I guess that was why I let you
get away with as much as you did. I wanted to believe
badly of you, but it was hard—bloody hard, when
everything about you——'

'Oh, Michael——'

'No, listen to me, Sara. I like you. You have spirit,
and I like that. I've never met a girl quite like you before. Don't leave me, Sara. Not until we—know one another better.'

Sara was unnerved by his declaration, unnerved, and
yet tantalised. She wanted so much to believe him, she
realised, but she knew it was all a charade. He didn't
know her. He only thought he did. And once he found
out . . .

'I'm sorry,' she said now, avoiding his gaze. 'I—I'm
flattered, of course, but——'

'Damn you, can't you forget what happened last
night?' he swore angrily. 'Can't you forget that I
thought you were Diane, and understand what I'm trying to tell you? I'm not the kind of man you think I
am. I have been a swine, I admit it. But letting you go
last night was not in my normal scheme of things, believe me. But you—well, you made me discover a side
of myself I didn't even know existed. Can't you at least

let me try and live with that discovery? Let me find out for myself—for both of us—what it means?'

Sara hesitated. 'I—I think you're presupposing something here,' she said carefully, though the words were more painful than any she had ever said. 'You—you're presupposing that—that I want to get to know you.'

'And don't you?' he demanded harshly. 'You're telling me that response I evoked last night is your normal reaction to a man who's trying to—ravish you?'

'Yes—I mean *no*! Oh, that's not the point.'

'What is the point, then?'

'I—well, you know nothing about me. I mean, I might not be as—as innocent as you think.' Sara flushed. 'I mean——' this was awful, and she hated lying to him, but her position had to be less tenuous; 'I am twenty-two, you know. I have—known other men.'

His expression hardened at this, but he did not let her go. Instead he said flatly: 'Well—good. I never did much like virgins anyway.'

She tore her hands from his then, although she suspected their freedom was as much through his choice as her strength. She had never been so shocked, or so exhilarated, but she could not let him go on.

'I have to go back to London,' she insisted stubbornly, and saw the look of impatience that narrowed his eyes.

'I see.' He flexed his shoulder muscles, watching her intently. 'And what will you tell Diane? That her little ploy worked? That the dynamite has been defused, and there's no further danger to herself?'

'Diane?' Sara licked her dry lips. In all the excitement she had forgotten the reasons why she was here.

Forgotten that Diane had sent her here, uncaring of the effects it might have on her health.

'Yes, Diane.' Michael pressed the point home. 'I should imagine she'll find this whole incident very—amusing.'

'Amusing?' Sara gazed at him, and he nodded.

'Why not?' His eyes were burning amber. 'After all, it's not every day a girl is prepared to risk her—doubtful virginity to protect her best friend!'

Sara's face flamed. 'She's not my best friend——'

'And you say you're not a virgin. Although I beg leave to doubt that,' he mocked.

'Besides, she wouldn't expect you to—to——'

'What?' His eyes glinted. 'Seduce you? No, probably not.'

'Well then . . .'

'I offered her much worse.'

'What do you mean?' Sara's eyes were wary as her earlier fears were realised. 'What—what did you say in that letter?'

Michael hesitated. Then he said quietly: 'Does it really matter? It was enough to frighten her. And she used you as her Judas sheep!'

Sara winced. Put like that it sounded so cold, so callous, so unfeeling. Diane had treated her as she had treated Adam—and there was nothing she could do about it.

Or was there? Surely the last thing Diane would expect her to do was to remain at Ravens Mill. No doubt she assumed Sara would return to London post-haste, bearing Adam's message with her, eager for explanations. She probably thought she could neutralise Sara's objections as easily as Sara herself had neutralised Adam's, and perhaps if it had been her husband waiting at Ravens Mill, her plans would have succeeded.

But Adam was dead, a fact that Diane did not know, and *would* not know until she, Sara, broke the news to her. What if Sara did not contact her? What if she let Diane sweat it out, as she had had to do? Let her suffer the pangs of anxiety, and possibly remorse? Let her wait and wonder, and worry what Adam might have done to her young associate?

Michael had been watching the play of emotions across her young face with a curious expression in his eyes. Now he heaved a heavy sigh and said flatly: 'All right. If you won't let me persuade you——'

'No! Wait!' Sara put out a hand, withdrawing it again abruptly when it contacted the fine wool of his dark grey sweater. 'I mean—I—I don't know. I—I might stay——'

Michael's long lashes came to veil his eyes. 'Why?' he demanded now. 'What has motivated your change of heart? Pity?'

'Pity?' she gasped. 'Of course not. Not for you, any-way. For myself perhaps.' She paused, drawing herself up with trembling dignity. 'What—what you said about Diane—I—I believe you.' She swallowed con-vulsively. 'If—if I return to London, I would have to tell her that—that Adam is dead. Why—why should I do that?'

A trace of admiration lifted the corners of his mouth. 'Why indeed?'

'I mean, why should I let her—let her off the hook?'

'You don't have to convince me,' Michael retorted dryly, and her pulses raced at the recklessness she was feeling.

'But,' she continued carefully, 'if—if I do stay here——'

'Conditions?' he enquired shortly, and she felt the familiar constriction in her chest that warned she had not had her medication that morning.

'There—there have to be—certain arrangements made,' she insisted. 'We—that is, if I do stay here, I—I intend to work.'

'I'm not arguing with that, am I?'

'And—and of course——'

'For God's sake!' his patience gave out. 'I know what you're going to say, and there's no need. Haven't I told you? You have nothing to fear from me. You don't imagine I'd force myself on you, do you? All I suggested was that we should get to know one another. If you find you can't go along with that, then just forget I'm here!' And without another word he left her, striding out through the open door and slamming it noisily behind him.

Forget he was here! Sara's mouth was dry, as she silently repeated his words. She wondered what he would say if she told him it was not he who frightened her, but *herself*, the abandoned being who had welcomed his lovemaking the night before and whose demands might not always be controllable. Diane had taken a risk by sending her here, but she was taking a bigger risk by remaining. Would he still want her to stay if he found out she was not the robust young woman he imagined her to be? What would his reactions be if he discovered her secret? And why was it so important to her that he should not find out?

CHAPTER FIVE

SARA was given a room in the west wing. Although it was on the landward side of the house, because of the vagaries of the coastline she could see the Atlantic breakers from her windows, coiling and swelling, and spitting their foam on to the ragged needle rocks. To the immediate west, the barren sweep of moorland was no more inviting, but with the sun turning its gorse-strewn slopes to gold, it had a stark beauty. She wondered where the house had got its name. There seemed nothing here to warrant the need for a mill, and certainly there was no mill-race rushing down into the boiling waters below the house.

The room which Mrs Penworthy had prepared for her was infinitely more appealing. It was old-fashioned, like the rest of the house, but the sprigged wallpaper and pastel-shaded curtains and coverlet seemed to indicate a more feminine touch. There was a chintz skirt on the dressing table, and a set of brushes with a *petit-point* motif, and the drawers were all scented with a distinctive perfume. Sara wondered whose room it had been. Diane's perhaps? But she discounted this supposition. Diane would never use such a simple fragrance.

Michael had carried her luggage upstairs, and then left her to her own devices. She didn't know where he was, although she thought she had heard a car start up somewhere near the house after he had deposited her cases without ceremony on the bed. He had not looked at her as she stood hesitantly by the window and she had made no attempt to speak to him in this curiously withdrawn mood.

Unpacking her belongings, she was again plagued with doubts as to the wisdom of what she was doing. It was all very well feeling resentment towards Diane, but was she behaving any more sensibly by staying, by risking another encounter such as the one she and Michael had had the night before? Apart from everything else, there was the growing awareness of what could result from such an encounter. If Michael had made love to her, without any thought of the outcome, she might have become pregnant. Pregnant! Her heart palpitated, and she grasped one of the bedposts for support. What would her doctor say to that? He had always maintained that she should avoid stress, and what was having a baby, if not stressful? She had no doubt that had Doctor Harding suspected that she might get seriously involved with some man, he would have warned her of the dangers of having children. But as she had never given him any cause for concern in that direction, naturally the subject had not really been considered. Like her mother, Doctor Harding had never encouraged her to get married, and anyone— any man, that was—who learned of her condition soon lost interest.

Her arched brows drawing together, she moved to stand in front of the leaved mirrors of the dressing table. She saw a slim girl, though not painfully so, with high cheekbones and a generous mouth. The lower lip was slightly fuller than the upper one, a sensuous detail, though she was unaware of it, which matched the sultry darkness of green eyes, sheltering behind sweeping golden dashes. Her hair was long and silky, almost as pale as her face, the only revealing characteristic of her whole make-up. Men had been attracted to her in the past, but her mother had always been around to fend them off, to warn them of her fragility—and lock her inside the ivory tower of her weakness, like some delicate Sleeping Beauty, just waiting for her prince to appear and break the magic spell. But no prince appeared; only Tony, with his predictable approach, and his equally predictable reaction to the truth.

Putting up both hands, she lifted her hair off her neck in an uncharacteristically defiant gesture. The movement sent her firm breasts surging against the thin silk of her shirt, outlining their fullness in curiously satisfying detail. She *was* reasonably attractive, she told herself half defensively, totally unaware of her own sensuality, only needing the reassurance that Michael had not been lying to her. She wasn't beautiful, like Diane, she thought, whose skin had a rosy glow, and whose hair was more yellow than gold. But she did have nice eyes, and her legs were quite good . . .

With a feeling of frustration she dropped her arms and turned away from the mirror. What was the point of pretending? she asked herself impatiently. She couldn't compete with Diane, and her health made it impossible for her to try. She was acting like a schoolgirl, wishing for the moon, and the sooner she came down to earth and faced reality, the better. Michael wouldn't send her away, particularly if she told him the truth; but why, oh, why didn't she want to stay on those terms? She was more like Cinderella than the Sleeping Beauty, she decided wryly. Living on borrowed time, waiting for midnight to strike.

A tap on her door brought her round with a start, her pulses, as usual, reacting like frightened rabbits'.

'Y-yes?' she called, fighting the constriction in her throat. 'Who—who is it?'

'Only me, miss.' The door opened and Mrs Penworthy appeared, carrying a tray. 'I thought you might like some coffee, seeing as how you didn't touch your breakfast. And what time would you like your lunch?'

Sara was grateful for her consideration. 'Coffee!' she exclaimed. 'That's exactly what I need. And—and I'll have lunch whenever Mr Tregower is ready.'

'Ah ...' Mrs Penworthy set down the tray on the folding table in the window embrasure. 'Mr Tregower may not be back for lunch, miss. Didn't he tell you? He's away over to Falmouth to see Mr Adam's solicitor.'

'Oh!' Sara absorbed this with what she hoped was casual interest. 'He—er—he may have mentioned it.' Looking down at the tray, she added: 'Did he also tell you I intend to work while I'm here? I wondered—is there a desk in the house, other than in—in the library?'

Mrs Penworthy looked doubtful. 'Well, there's Mr Adam's study, miss. That's never used these days. I suppose you might use that, but you'd have to ask Mr Tregower first.'

'Of course.' Sara nodded, fingering the spoon in its saucer, noticing that although Mrs Penworthy called Diane's late husband by his name, she always said *Mr* Tregower, when she spoke of Michael. She wondered why. Was that really his name? If he was born on the wrong side of the blanket, as he maintained, might his name not be something else entirely?

'What kind of work were you thinking of doing, miss?' enquired Mrs Penworthy, no doubt emboldened, Sara thought wryly, by her own timid attitude.

'I write,' she said now, lifting her head and looking the woman squarely in the eyes. 'I'm writing a book.'

'Is that so?' Mrs Penworthy was evidently impressed. 'Well now, isn't that interesting? A writer! You should have met Mr Adam's wife. She's an actress, you know. Quite a famous one, so I'm told. You and she would have got along famously, having so much in common.'

Sara bent her head. So Michael had not mentioned who she was. Only her name, and that she was a friend of his, no doubt. She wondered what Mrs Penworthy really imagined their relationship to be. She had obviously surprised her when she told her she had come there to work. But had Michael been able to convince the housekeeper that her arrival had been as unexpected as he maintained?

'I don't think so,' she said now, in answer to the woman's probing observation. 'Writers are not like actresses, Mrs Penworthy. They like their—privacy. They don't seek the limelight. At least, not usually.'

'I expect some do and some don't,' retorted the housekeeper, her sharp eyes darting round the room as she spoke, taking in the tumble of Sara's lingerie upon the bed, the woollens and pants that littered her opened cases. 'Should I finish unpacking for you?'

'Oh—no, thank you.' This time Sara's tone was firm. 'I can manage.'

'Very well, miss.' Almost regretfully, Mrs Penworthy picked up a smoky-blue cashmere sweater and smoothed it over her arm. 'This is pretty, isn't it? But I can't help noticing you don't appear to have brought many dresses with you. Now, if there's anything you want pressing, you have only to say.'

'Thank you, but I came here for a working holiday, Mrs Penworthy, not to be entertained.' Sara had difficulty in keeping her tone polite. 'Now, I think if we have lunch at one o'clock, that should give—Mr Tregower time to get back if he's coming, don't you?'

It was a dismissal, and Mrs Penworthy took it, but after she had gone Sara was not surprised to find she was shaking. She had never dismissed anybody before, and the relief was unnerving. Even so, she felt impatient with her own inadequacy. After all, the woman had only been curious, and who could blame her? Living in a place like this as she was, there was bound to be speculation.

Nevertheless, Sara couldn't prevent the impulse to push the cashmere sweater to the back of the drawer, and she quickly disposed of the rest of her clothes before Mrs Penworthy returned for the tray.

Michael had not returned at lunch time, and Sara ate a silent meal in the room where he had baited her over dinner the night before. In daylight, she could see the scars of long usage on the furniture, and the worn tapestry of the chairs, and she thought how sad it was that the house should be abandoned now, when for years it had been home to generations of Tregowers. Was it Diane's now, in truth, or were there other relatives to be contacted? She doubted Michael would ever want to live here, and given half a chance, she guessed Diane would sell it.

Diane! Everything seemed to come back to Diane, she thought irritably, getting up from the table without doing real justice to Mrs Penworthy's Cornish pasty. Why couldn't she put the other girl out of her mind and concentrate on the reasons why she had agreed to come to Cornwall in the first place?

Deciding some fresh air was what she needed, she went upstairs to change, coming down again warmly attired, with dark red woollen pants tucked into knee-length suede boots. Her dark blue sweater was hidden beneath a grey sheepskin jacket, whose hem and hood were attractively edged with grey and white flecked fur. With her pale silky hair escaping from the sides of the hood, she felt reasonably satisfied with her appearance, but as Michael was not around, there was no one to observe her departure.

The wind had risen again, bringing a bite to the temperature that in turn whipped colour into her otherwise pale cheeks. Someone, Michael she guessed, had moved the Mini around the side of the house, and although she was tempted to revise her original plan of going for a walk, she refused to give in to what she told herself was a purely lazy impulse. After all, walking was good for her, so long as she didn't walk too far, and the salty taste of the air was invigorating.

Beyond the overgrown garden the cliffs fell away to a sheltered cove, which in summer was probably very appealing. A winding path seemed to give access to the cove, but it was too steep for Sara to tackle, even had she wanted to. Inland, she could see the coast road, also winding down to sea level, and the cluster of cottages that must be Torleven. There were one or two fishing boats out in the bay, and others bobbing about near the harbour. She could even see some drawn up on to the shingle, which would also float when the tide came in. At present the ocean was receding, drawing back upon itself, exposing the ugly rocks that could tear a ship's keel to shreds. And probably had, too, Sara guessed, grimacing as she remembered the tales she had read. A wrecker's coast, this, with many a vessel floundering on these rocks, lured into the deadly harbour by a treacherous light.

Turning back from the cliffs, she surveyed the house behind her. It was still stark and forbidding, without any of the gentling touches of ivy or Virginia creeper, but, now she had spent a night within its walls, it was no longer the unfamiliar place it had been. She could even pick out the windows of her room, and the imposing façade that fronted the master bedroom, where she had slept the night before.

Picking her way along the cliffs, she watched the sea-birds swooping and diving in their continuous search for food. Gannets and guillemots, terns and gulls, their screeching cries carrying on the wind, they offered their objections to this invader into their territory, and after a while Sara turned inland, away from their noisy clamour.

The moors offered less variety, but were infinitely more peaceful. Stretches of rough turf, hillocks, and gorse, and wind-torn stunted vegetation. There didn't appear to be a house for miles, and the further she came from Ravens Mill the easier it was to believe she had actually stepped back in time. Shades of *Jamaica Inn*, she thought wryly, realising that if Joss Merlyn himself had come riding across the moor towards her, she would hardly have been surprised.

Once, she thought she saw a fox. The reddish-brown body slunk away into the undergrowth at her approach, but she was sure she had startled it as much as it had startled her. She saw a number of rabbit holes, twisting her ankle in one of them, and guessed the wily predator would not go short of food here.

The sun had lost all heat by the time she turned back to Ravens Mill. It wasn't late, but it was still early in the year, and it had been a particularly cold spring. Her fingertips were frozen, but her feet were warm enough in the thick boots, and she thrust her gloved hands into the pockets of her sheepskin jacket.

Trudging back towards the house, she wondered if Michael had returned. No doubt he had by now, and her heart warned her of the effect even thinking of him had on her. During the walk, she had achieved a certain detachment from the more personal aspects of her situation, but the prospect of meeting Michael again drove all other thoughts from her head.

The ankle she had twisted was aching by the time she reached the fenced boundary that marked the immediate surroundings of Ravens Mill, and the walk had tired her more than she had anticipated. Truthfully, she had felt perfectly fit until she started to think about Michael, and she guessed it was emotion that had sapped her strength.

However, she was given little chance to recover from the exercise. As she came through the shrubbery towards the house, the man she had been thinking about came striding towards her, his face and demeanour indicating more than a casual interest in her whereabouts.

'Where the hell have you been?' he snapped, grasping her elbows and subjecting her to an angry appraisal. 'I thought you said you came here to work! For God's sake, I thought you must have gone down to the cove and been swept out on the tide!'

'I'm sorry.' Sara swayed a little as he set her free, and his anger quickly turned to reluctant concern.

'What is it? Are you all right? Did I hurt you or something?'

'No.' Sara endeavoured to appear calm. 'I—er—I twisted my ankle, that's all. It's nothing, just a sprain.'

'Is it?'

Michael sounded less than convinced, and with a muttered oath he swung her up into his arms, as he had done the night before, and began to carry her towards the house.

Sara made a paltry attempt to prevent him, but in truth she was glad of his strength. Even so, the warmth of his breath fanning her forehead was disturbing, and she wondered if walking the rest of the way to the house would have been any more exhausting. She was supremely conscious of him, of the width of his shoulder beneath her hand, of the hardness of his chest, and the firm easy strides he took, that brought them to the porch in only a few seconds. Their breath mingled in the cold air, his mildly scented with the tobacco he smoked, and hers short and laboured, evidence of the weakness that persisted in making itself felt.

He didn't put her down in the hall, as she had expected. Instead, he carried her into the library and set her on her feet in front of the roaring fire, allowing her body to slide the length of his with disruptive consequences.

'You're frozen,' he accused, and his voice was husky. 'Why the devil didn't you tell me, if you wanted to go out? You could have come to Falmouth. We could have had lunch together.'

Sara drew an unsteady breath. 'I—I wanted to walk,' she declared, loosening her hood and allowing her hair to spill out like a pale cloud. 'And—and there's no need for you to be concerned about me. I'm perfectly capable of taking care of myself.'

'The hell you are!' As she determinedly concentrated on unfastening the leather buttons of her jacket, Michael paced across the room, combing impatient fingers through his hair. 'Don't you know the moors are dangerous?. There are pools out there, and marshland, and bogs—that can suck you down in seconds!'

'Oh, really ...' Sara lifted her head and gazed at him. 'You're only trying to frighten me! I doubt very much whether there's a marsh within twenty miles of here!'

Michael met her gaze aggressively, but she was not convinced by the insolent lift of his eyebrows. Shaking her head, she bent to warm her hands at the blaze, and his resentment exploded into action.

'What do you know about it?' he demanded, crossing the room and glaring down at her. 'Were you brought up on these moors? Did you learn every rock and gully of these cliffs before you were ten years old?'

Reluctantly, Sara straightened. 'Did you?'

'Yes, I did, damn you, and I know what's out there better than you do!'

'All right.' Sara made a gesture of resignation. 'I'm sorry. I've said that once, and I'll say it again. How was I to know I was expected to remain in the house? I must say—if—if you hadn't been here, I should have had to fend for myself, so——'

'So—nothing!' he muttered, breathing heavily, and then, almost compulsively it seemed, his hands reached for her. They slid over her shoulders and around the back of her neck, beneath the silken curtain of her hair, compelling her towards him. His hands were cold but insistent, the lapels of his brown corded jacket parting as he moved to expose the dark shadow of hair, visible beneath the fine cream silk of his shirt. He had pulled down the brown knitted tie during the altercation which had just taken place, and it was suspended before her eyes like some hypnotic pendulum, riveting her gaze and inducing the same lethargy she had felt the night before. It was doubly disturbing when she remembered she had seen him without the confining influence of his clothes, and she had to fight the longing to succumb to his attraction.

'*No!*' she choked, and with a superhuman effort she twisted out of his embrace, putting the width of the hearthrug between them, gazing at him with darkly tormented eyes. 'You—you promised!'

Judging by the pallor he was exhibiting now beneath his tan, Michael was no less disturbed than she was, but his lips tightened when he met her accusing stare. 'Yes, of course,' he got out stiffly, running unsteady fingers round the inside of his collar. 'It's I who should apologise, as you say. I'm afraid I—but never mind.' He expelled a harsh breath, before adding with politeness: 'I'll get you a drink. Something to warm you up. Or would you prefer tea?'

Sara moistened her dry lips. It had been a dangerous moment, and she knew she would have to avoid such moments in future if she wanted to convince him she meant what she said. When his hands had touched her, when his fingers had caressed the lobes of her ears, she had known an almost overwhelming urge to press herself against him, and if he had kissed her ...

'I—tea would be very nice,' she said now, her voice low and controlled. 'Perhaps—perhaps I could have it in my room. I'd like to—to rest my ankle for a while.'

'Rest here,' suggested Michael bleakly. 'That chair behind you is very comfortable, and there's a footstool you can use.'

Sara hesitated. 'I—won't I be in your way?'

Michael's mouth turned down at the corners. 'No,' he declared tersely, 'you won't be in my way.'

'Very well.' Sara delayed only another moment before sliding her jacket off her shoulders and looking round nervously for somewhere to put it.

'Give that to me.'

Michael took the sheepskin from her, and then strode towards the door and disappeared into the hall. Sara looked after him, and then, with a doubtful shrug, she subsided into the soft velvet armchair beside the fire. It was warmer here, she told herself, in defence of her submission, but it had a hollow ring. Nevertheless, if she was to stay here, a state of neutrality must be encouraged between them, and not the kind of armed provocation which could so easily lead to open conflict.

Mrs Penworthy brought the tea on a trolley. She wheeled it into the library and set it close to Sara's chair, her inquisitive gaze taking in the girl's boots, removed now and lying carelessly on the hearth, her toes curled on the fireside fender.

'Mr Tregower tells me you've twisted your ankle,' she remarked, and Sara made an offhand gesture.

'Just slightly,' she assured her quickly. 'It's not serious. I probably put my foot down a rabbit hole.'

'You've been walking then, have you, miss? On the moor? Yes, it's quite brisk out there at this time of the year.'

Sara nodded, not quite knowing how to reply, and Mrs Penworthy went on: 'Mr Tregower's mother, she used to like walking on the moor, she did. But then that's natural, isn't it? Them being travelling folk, and all.'

'Thank you, Mrs Penworthy, that will do!'

Michael's voice behind her was cold as ice, and Sara had scarcely time to formulate what the housekeeper had been saying before she had made some mumbled apology and left the room.

Michael himself lowered the footstool he had been carrying on to the hearthrug at her feet, then seated himself opposite. It was a round footstool, with cabriole legs, and although its tapestry cover was worn, Sara guessed it was probably quite valuable.

'It belonged to Adam's mother,' Michael remarked, aware of her interest. 'She used it a lot, I believe. She was never a robust woman.'

'No?' Sara hoped her response was not too faint. 'Er—what was wrong with her?'

Michael shrugged, resting his dark head back against the wine velvet upholstery of his chair. 'I believe she suffered from anaemia initially, and later, after having Adam, she developed leukaemia. She died just after I was born.'

'Just—after——' Sara hoped her response was not too revealing. 'But you had different mothers.'

'As Mrs Penworthy was just relating,' observed Michael dryly. 'Shall we have some tea?'

'What? Oh—oh, yes.' Sara turned awkwardly to the trolley. 'Er—milk and sugar?'

'Please.' He sat up, spreading his legs and allowing his hands to hang between. 'How's the ankle?'

'It's not painful.' Sara handed him his cup, trying not to let it rattle in the saucer. 'I don't think I've really sprained it. Just twisted it, as I said.'

'Good.' He raised his cup to his lips and took a mouthful of the hot beverage. 'I'd hate you to suffer some serious injury while you're here.'

His tone was mocking, but she refused to rise to the bait. Instead she gave her attention to the dish of scones Mrs Penworthy had also provided, finding her appetite was healthier now than it had been at lunch time. Was that because of her walk, or because of

nerves? Either way, she enjoyed the crisp shells with
their soft warm centres, spreading them liberally with
jam and cream when Michael refused to join her.

'Is your room to your liking?'

It was Michael who broke the silence that had fallen
between them, and she wiped her sticky fingers on her
napkin before replying.

'It's—very nice,' she conceded carefully. 'Rather—
unexpected.'

'Unexpected?' He frowned.

'It's so—feminine.' She flushed. 'I suppose it must
have been Mrs Tregower's room.'

'Which Mrs Tregower do you mean?'

He was not being very helpful, lying back in his
chair again, surveying her through those thick curling
lashes. Relaxed, as he was now, his eyes were almost
hazel, but she knew when anger sparked their depths,
they could turn to molten gold.

'Why, your—your—*Adam's* mother,' she offered uncomfortably. 'I know Diane wouldn't have chosen anything so—so—unsophisticated.'

'No?'

Sara sighed. 'No,' she said firmly. 'Besides, she—she
would share your brother's room, wouldn't she?' She
paused. 'It—it wasn't Diane's room, was it?'

There was another pregnant silence, until at last
Michael conceded the truth of her statement. 'No,' he
agreed, 'it wasn't Diane's room. But then it wasn't
Adam's mother's room either.'

'Oh!' Sara's colour mounted. 'Then—then whose?'

There was a glint of amber between the dark lashes.
'Can't you guess?'

Sara put her hands over the arms of the chair, grip-
ping them tightly. 'Your—mother's?' she ventured

slowly, and at the inclination of his head: 'But how could that be? You said——'

Michael's expression was unrevealing. 'What? That I was born before old Adelaide died?' His lips twisted. 'You know how these things happen. You should!'

'Of course I know.' Sara's face burned. 'I only meant —that is—it's unusual, isn't it? Your—your mother living in the house while—while Mr Tregower's wife was alive.'

'I didn't say she was.'

Michael was annoyingly obtuse, and she stared frustratedly at him. 'But you——'

'I agreed that the room you are using used to be my mother's room. It did. But after Adelaide was dead.'

Sara was puzzled. 'But if his wife was—dead——'

'Why didn't he marry her, you mean?' Michael's tone was dry. 'Instead of keeping her as his mistress?'

Sara drew an uneven breath. 'It—it's really nothing to do with me.'

'Isn't it?' Michael's expression was mocking. 'So why were you listening so avidly to old Mother Penworthy's gossip?'

'I wasn't.' Sara was indignant. 'I—she was talking to me. I didn't encourage her. Besides,' she faced him defiantly, 'you shouldn't have been eavesdropping.'

For an awful moment she thought she had gone too far. He levered himself up from his lounging position and stared at her unsmilingly. The amber eyes were brilliant now, no longer sleepily dormant, and the lines beside his mouth were sharply etched in his tanned skin. Then, when the knuckles of her fingers were showing white and her heart was hammering in her ears, a faint smile of admiration touched his lips.

'*Touché*,' he commented, holding her eyes with his.

'Whoever would have thought such pale beauty could hide such latent fire?'

Sara's fingers went limp and she sank back against the unholstery. These emotional confrontations were sapping her energies, and with inert fingers she reached for her teacup, finding a minute amount of revitalisation from the sweetened liquid. But the strain of the last few minutes had imprinted itself on her face, and Michael viewed with some concern the darkening circles around her eyes.

'Are you all right?' he asked, watching her intently. 'You look—drained suddenly. What did I say? I don't terrify you, do I?'

'Of course not.' Sara's response was breathy, and not at all convincing, and he frowned.

'What is it with you? Sometimes you seem—oh, I don't know—so—fragile! Like crystal. And with as many facets.'

Sara replaced her cup on the trolley. 'I'm sorry——'

'And stop apologising to me, every time I make a careless comment.' He rose abruptly to his feet, turning to the mantel and resting his balled fists upon it. 'Either you're extremely naïve, or extremely clever. I can't honestly determine which.'

'Can't you?'

It was all Sara could get out, but it seemed to galvanise his argument. 'No,' he declared harshly. 'Oh, I don't know if you are sexually innocent, but anyway innocence is more than a physical thing; it's a state of mind. And God help me, I've never met anyone like you before!'

Sara moved her shoulders in a helpless gesture. There was little she could say in the face of his frustration, particularly as his words were a little too close for comfort. But the last thing she wanted was to make him suspicious of her, and swinging her feet off the footstool, she said:

'I think I really will go to my room now, if you don't mind. I'd like a shower before—before dinner, and I have one or two personal things to attend to——'

'Wait!' He swung round to face her, his eyes searching and appealing at the same time. 'You might as well hear the rest of the story from me as glean it in snatches from her ...' His meaning was clear, but he paused before going on: 'You've heard of the travelling people, haven't you? You knew what Mrs Penworthy meant?'

Sara shook her head. 'Honestly, this isn't at all necessary——' she began, but he interrupted her.

'Let me be the judge of that.' His mouth was grim. 'You might as well know who attempted to seduce you.'

Sara allowed a faint sigh to escape her lips. 'So— your mother was a gipsy.'

'Yes, she was.'

'She's dead?'

'That's right.' He paused. 'She died on the moor. Of exposure, they said. She was running away from my father at the time.'

His statement was delivered in an almost expressionless voice, but Sara sensed how angry it made him. It gave birth to a dozen other questions, but she also knew she had no right to ask them. The facile words of sympathy hovered on her lips, but were never spoken. He had not told her because he wanted her sympathy, but she wondered if he was aware of the revealing tightening of his fingers around her wrist.

'So you see why I was so furious when I found you'd disappeared this afternoon,' he said in a low voice.

'Even though our relationship is so different. My mother wouldn't marry my father, you see.'

Sara's lips parted involuntarily. 'Oh, but—I mean—you're wrong! Why, your mother lived in this house. You said so.'

'Not voluntarily, believe me. But when her own father found she was pregnant, he turned her out. My father found her lodgings in the village until after I was born. She was helpless, you see. She had no relatives to help her, no money. He kept her, and me, until Adelaide died. Then he brought us back to Ravens Mill.'

'I see.' Sara caught her lower lip between her teeth. 'And—and after she died?'

Michael's mouth thinned. 'I was sent to boarding schools until I was old enough to go to university. Then, as I told you, he despatched me to Coimbra.'

'And—and Adam?'

As if he became aware of the deadly grip he had on her wrist, his fingers slackened, and she drew her arm away, rubbing the circulation back into her veins.

'Adam?' He heaved a sigh. 'Adam and I had been very close. Unlike the fictional hostilities that usually exist between half-brothers, we had a good relationship. He felt it as strongly as I did when I was sent away.'

'He—he was older,' she ventured, and Michael nodded.

'Yes, five years older. But in some ways I always felt years older than him. I guess it's my—Romany ancestry. I'm quite a mixture, am I not? One quarter Portuguese, one quarter Cornish, and half Romany. Quite a handful for any child!'

Sara felt the colour returning to her cheeks at his words. It was as if he had read her thoughts. She pressed her lips together and forced such disruptive speculations aside.

'May I go to my room now?' she asked, only to find his tawny eyes raking her with evident exasperation.

'Is that all you have to say?' he demanded. 'Doesn't it bother you? You might have felt differently, if there'd been any risk of you becoming pregnant.'

'It—it wouldn't have been very likely,' she suggested jerkily. 'I mean——'

'There's always that possibility.'

'Then—then it's fortunate——'

'Yes, isn't it?' But his eyes were broading. 'Particularly as I would never abandon any child of mine.'

'As—as your father did, you mean?' Sara's mouth was dry. 'But surely—he paid for your education.'

'And do you consider that's enough? To *pay* for a child's upbringing? What about its feelings? Its emotions? Its need to feel wanted in this harsh, primitive world we've created?'

Sara bent her head. 'What are you saying? That I would have no choice in the matter? That—that you would bring up this—this hypothetical child, without any assistance from me?'

'No.' His hand grasped her chin and jerked it upwards, forcing her to look at him. 'I'm saying that if you were pregnant, there would be no question. I would marry you. No child of mine is ever going to be a bastard. Do I make myself clear?'

Sara tried to lift her chin out of his grasp, but she couldn't do it, and her voice was shaky as she said: 'You're very sure of yourself.' Her tongue appeared, to circle her lips. 'What if the woman you chose refused to marry you? Women do bring up children alone, you know.'

'I should make her,' he said simply. 'One way or the other,' and she knew he would.

CHAPTER SIX

THE room which had been Adam Tregower's study overlooked the Atlantic. Beyond the tangled wasteland of the garden, the craggy outline of the cliffs formed an uneven frame for the constantly-moving turmoil of the ocean, and with the advent of spring, probing fingers of vegetation were bringing their own colour to the barren landscape.

Seated at the desk where Adam had attended to the business of his estate, Sara had spent some time just gazing at the view, trying to instil herself with feelings of inspiration, but they simply would not come. For several days now her book had lain in front of her, like some tender virgin waiting to be ravished, she thought wryly, using the metaphor with deliberate irony, but she had not written one word or edited one line of the manuscript. She was completely devoid of all ideas concerning her story, and any distraction, any sound in the house, magnified by her over-sensitised condition, sent her eyes darting enviously towards the closed door of her self-imposed prison. All her plans of completing the second draft within the first week had had to be abandoned, and all she could hope now was that Michael should not suspect her longing to be with him.

Since their conversation in the library she had seen little of him. At dinner that same evening, she had broached the subject of finding somewhere to work, and as Mrs Penworthy had predicted, he had offered her the study. Since then she had only seen him at mealtimes, and latterly not always then. Occasionally he had been absent, and Mrs Penworthy had delivered his apologies, accompanying them with snatches of gossip Sara would rather not have heard.

'I believe he's gone over to the riding stables,' she offered on one such occasion. 'They say Mrs Morton, she runs the riding stables, you know, is an old friend of Mr Tregower's! Used to know him years ago, so they say, before she married.'

And at dinner the night before—'Mr Tregower said to tell you he'd be dining with the Gwithians this evening. Doctor Gwithian is our local G.P. and I heard that his twin daughters are just home from the university.'

The information was well meant, Sara told herself, trying to be generous, but the fact remained that it did not help her concentration. It was all very well trying to dismiss what had happened between herself and Michael, but still she couldn't prevent the twinges of resentment she experienced when she heard of his association with other women. It was ridiculous, particularly as she had no hold on him, *nor wanted to have*, she averred fiercely, but the feelings persisted. It hurt, too, that there had still been no word from Diane, not even a telephone call to find out if she was all right, and the schedules she had set herself became hollow things at best beside the unexpected uncertainty of her present position.

So far, at least, hiding her condition had proved no obstacle. They were virtually living separate lives, just as she had demanded. What worried her most was her own reactions to this unsatisfactory situation. Instead of getting on with what she had planned to do, she spent her time daydreaming, wasting her break from routine in hopeless preoccupation. And after Mrs Penworthy had left for home in the evenings, the nights stretched ahead of her, lonely and unexciting.

At lunch time she had the unexpected company of her host.

He came into the dining room as Mrs Penworthy was ladling soup into Sara's bowl, his hair damp, from a sea mist which was blowing inland, the scent of horses clinging about his leather jacket and tight-fitting jeans. His presence immediately electrified the previously dormant atmosphere in the room, stimulating her senses and sending the blood surging pleasurably along her veins. He was so virile, so masculine, so obviously full of life and energy, that unwittingly her gaze mirrored a little of the envy she was feeling.

However, Michael's lips twisted at her wide-eyed glance, and he put another interpretation on the wistful wrinkle of her nose. 'Forgive me,' he remarked mockingly, brushing back his hair with a careless hand. 'I forgot to change. I keep forgetting I have a visitor in the house.'

Sara crumbled the roll on her plate with nervous fingers. 'I'm sure you hadn't forgotten,' she retorted, in a low voice, aware of Mrs Penworthy's interested attention. 'And—and your appearance is of no consequence to me.'

'No?' Michael took the chair opposite her, deliberately ignoring the place the housekeeper had hurriedly set for him at the end of the table. 'Mrs Penworthy,' he addressed himself to that lady, 'did you hear that? Our guest doesn't care how I present myself. Do you think she'd feel the same if I appeared stark naked?'

Mrs Penworthy tutted and gave an embarrassed laugh, while Sara sat in mortified silence, wishing the floor could open up and swallow her. He was obviously in a tormenting mood, and she should have known better than to cross swords with him in the first place.

However, as soon as Mrs Penworthy left the room she found herself saying tersely: 'Why must you try to shock people? I haven't seen you in days, and when you do appear you seem to find enjoyment in—in making a fool of me.'

'I should have thought it was myself I was making a fool of,' he retorted shortly, helping himself to butter. 'What do you expect me to do? Apologise for living? I can't do that. I'm here—and you're going to have to live with that!'

'I'm not objecting to your presence, am I?' Sara held up her head. 'Only to the manner of its manifestation.'

Michael scowled. 'Such long words,' he sneered. 'What you mean is—don't come to my table smelling of the stables!'

Sara sighed. 'I—I like the smell of horses, as a matter of fact. That has nothing to do with this argument.'

'So why don't you come riding with me?'

Sara hesitated. 'Because—because I'm here to work. I told you.'

'To hell with your work!' Michael spooned soup into his mouth. 'I'm sick of hearing about it! You object to my joining you and making some small effort to lighten the mood in here, and all you can talk about is your *work*!'

Sara moved her shoulders in an offhand gesture. 'I didn't ask you to join me,' she began, but the look in his eyes made her draw back into her chair.

'No, you didn't,' he conceded harshly. 'And believe me, I thought twice before doing so.'

'Then——'

'Let me finish.' His black brows were drawn together

angrily. 'I've tried staying away. Or perhaps you haven't noticed. I've accepted every invitation I've been offered in the hope that you might show some reaction.' His lips curled. 'But no, nothing is said. You continue to go on with your life, as if I never existed.' He leant towards her. 'When I came in here today, I could tell from your expression that I'm the last person you wanted to see. So why do I do it? Why do I keep hammering my head against a brick wall? Because I know you, Sara. I've held your naked body in my arms, and felt your instant response. You're not as prim and proper as you appear, and that's why I keep trying to shock that virgin little soul of yours out of its apathy!'

Mrs Penworthy's reappearance with a leg of lamb, and a tray of vegetables, terminated his outburst, and Sara had time to regain her composure before the housekeeper departed again. They had neither of them done justice to the soup, and Mrs Penworthy's expression revealed her disapproval at this state of affairs.

'Was there something wrong with the broth?' she enquired, clattering the dishes together in evident annoyance, but Michael's candour easily disarmed her.

'It was delicious,' he assured her smilingly, and if Sara had not known better she would never have believed that only moments before he had been exhibiting an entirely different side of his character. He could be so charming, if he chose, and Mrs Penworthy was not proof against his undoubted expertise. 'But, as you know, I've been riding with Mrs Morton, and I have to confess, she offered me a drink afterwards.'

And what else? wondered Sara broodingly, hardly listening to the housekeeper's mock reproval. Mrs Morton, she thought dourly. The woman Michael had known since before he went to Brazil.

Michael carved the meat, and with Mrs Penworthy's departure Sara's nerves tightened. She didn't know how to deal with him in this mood, and she could tell by his expression that he had not forgotten what he had been saying earlier. Watching him slice the leg of lamb, her eyes were drawn to his hands, firm around the carving knife and fork he was using. Strong hands they were, capable hands; not the hands of an accountant, as Tony's had been, but hard and brown and muscular, yet with long sensitive fingers. She knew his fingers were sensitive, they had been sensitive when they touched her, and a wave of heat came out all over her body at the realisation of what she was thinking. Almost convulsively she dragged her eyes away, looking down at her own hands, sweating in her lap, and tried to compose herself. But when she looked up again she found he was watching her, and she had the unnerving impression that he knew exactly what she had been thinking.

'Yes,' he said, holding her eyes with his, deliberately allowing the thick black lashes to narrow his lids still further. 'You know you're not indifferent to me, and I wish you'd stop pretending that you are.'

Sara tore her gaze away. 'I don't know what you're talking about,' she exclaimed jerkily, reaching for the dish of vegetables. 'Do you think we could just finish the meal without any more argument? I—I have a lot to do this afternoon.'

'Do you?'

His tone was ominous, but Sara did not risk looking at him again. When he reseated himself, setting the dish of meat between them, she helped herself silently, concentrating on her plate to the exclusion of all else. She didn't know if he was eating anything. She didn't want to know. She only wanted to finish the meal and get out of the room, before he chose to prove to her exactly what a liar she was.

She almost jumped out of her skin when his chair was thrown back and he got to his feet and stalked out of the room. It was totally unexpected. She had not expected him to give up the battle so easily, and contrarily, now that he was gone, she felt ridiculously abandoned.

All interest in the food had disappeared, but she was loath to leave the table and permit Mrs Penworthy to make her own judgments. The housekeeper was too fond of gossip to allow that to happen, although what she could say to allay her speculation, she had no idea.

However, when the housekeeper did appear, she made no comment about the neglect of her meal. She gathered the unused plates without comment, and then, just as Sara was deciding that Michael's earlier statement had been sufficient explanation, she said:

'I'll be leaving after I've finished these dishes, Miss Fortune. It's my evening off, and I've spoken to Mr Tregower, and he says it will be all right if I leave a cold buffet for you to serve in the kitchen.'

'Oh!' Sara's lips parted hesitantly. 'Oh, yes, of course, Mrs Penworthy. Thank you.'

The housekeeper nodded. 'Can I get you anything else now? Apart from coffee, that is? Cheese and biscuits perhaps?'

Sara flushed, aware of her scarcely-touched plate. 'I—don't think so, thank you. I'm afraid I wasn't hungry either.'

Mrs Penworthy shrugged, and picked up the tray. 'It seems to me you spend too much time locked up in that study, if you don't mind me saying so,' she declared.

'Proper peaky, you look. You need some fresh air, if you ask me.'

Sara stiffened. 'But I didn't ask you, did I, Mrs Penworthy,' she stated. And then, impulsively: 'Did—did Mr Tregower ask you to tell this?'

'Mr Tregower?' The housekeeper frowned. 'Now why would he do a thing like that, miss?'

Sara got to her feet, realising how foolish she had been to suggest such a thing. 'I—why—oh, no reason, Mrs Penworthy. No reason at all.'

Of course she instantly regretted the carelessness of her words. They had been ill-considered, to say the least, and Mrs Penworthy had every reason to be regarding her in that speculative way. But it was too late now, and as the housekeeper turned away Sara could tell from her expression that she was intrigued. No doubt the peculiarities of their relationship would make an interesting topic of conversation in the Penworthy home that evening.

Annoyed with herself, and too restless to wait for her coffee, Sara left the dining room, hesitating in the hall when she saw that the library door was open. That door was usually closed, and she invariably spent her evenings in the small drawing room where Michael had carried her that first afternoon at Ravens Mill. Since Mrs Penworthy learned that she was to stay in the house, she had opened up several of the rooms, and the library, which Sara always associated with Michael anyway, was seldom used.

Giving in to another impulse, she moved to the doorway, drawing back instinctively when she saw Michael standing by the windows, staring out at the untended garden. His hands were thrust deep into the pockets of his jacket, and his expression, even in profile, was dark and brooding.

Unwilling to be found spying on him, Sara would have made a hasty retreat to the drawing room, when he rounded on his heel and saw her turning stealthily away. For a moment their eyes locked, and although Sara's lids dropped defensively, it was too late to pretend she hadn't seen him.

'Did you want something, Miss Fortune?' he asked, strolling towards her, mocking her name which everyone eventually made fun of. 'Did you enjoy your lunch? I imagine you found it much more to your taste after I left the room.'

Sara refused to rise to his baiting. 'I was just about to go to the study,' she said, conscious of the sheer animal magnetism about him. The rough silk shirt he wore beneath his corded jacket was open at the neck, and the darkness of the skin it exposed was accentuated by the glimpse of dark hair on his chest. With his hands in his pockets, the buttons of his shirt were stretched to their limits, and she tried not to look at the muscular flesh visible between. 'I—I'm sorry if I disturbed you.'

'You always disturb me, Sara,' he replied, his narrowed eyes dark and sensual. 'But you know that, don't you? That's why you continually wear these—boyish clothes!'

Sara cast a fleeting glance down at herself. The white shirt was certainly not boyish. Its full sleeves were very feminine, she thought, and although she had teamed it with matching pants and waistcoat, they too were made of velvet, hardly the material for a boy's wardrobe.

Looking up at him again, she was aware of the

quickened rise and fall of her breasts, which were anything but masculine, swollen by his provocation, and
revealingly taut.

'They're the only clothes I've got, I'm afraid,' she
said now, sheltering behind indignation. 'As I per-
sistently keep saying, I'm here to work——'

'Work!' He made it sound like a dirty word, stretching out a hand and flicking the lace-edged collar of her
shirt, so that she flinched away from his tormenting
fingers. 'And what work have you done?' he enquired,
turning back into the library, so that she was obliged to
follow him to hear what he was saying. Besides, she
was aware that Mrs Penworthy could be standing just
inside the dining room, listening to their conversation,
and with this in mind, she allowed the door to swing
to behind her. But not close completely. 'Tell me,' he
looked at her over his shoulder, 'have you telephoned
Diane yet? Have you reassured her that everything is
under control?'

'No!' Sara was really indignant now. 'If she wants to
know anything, she can ring me. I'd have expected her
to do so before now.'

'Would you?' Michael's mouth curled as he turned
fully to face her. 'Well—yes, perhaps you would. Innocent that you are!'

Sara tried to contain the revealing wave of colour
his words aroused, but it was a losing battle, and her
fists clenched in angry impotence. 'You don't know how
innocent I am,' she snapped, forgetting for the moment
that she was not supposed to get agitated.

'No, I don't, do I?' Michael's mouth hardened. 'And
you consistently remind me of the fact.'

'I?' Sara gasped. 'This is the first time I've mentioned
it!'

'You don't have to mention it,' he grated harshly. 'Just looking at you is a continual reminder.'

'Then don't look at me!' she exclaimed, though her knees quivered at the grimness of his expression.

'How can I help looking at you?' he retorted, his eyes dropping the length of her body with insolent emphasis. 'You fascinate me, do you know that? I keep remembering how you looked without those damn clothes, and in spite of all my good intentions I want to see you that way again.'

'No——'

'Yes.' He made no move towards her, but the twelve inches or so of space between them fairly crackled with electricity. 'I can't help it. You're beautiful—and I want you. I need you, Sara. Don't you care that you're tearing me to pieces?'

Sara gulped. 'You—you shouldn't say things like that——'

'Why not? They're the truth.' He moved his broad shoulders in a dismissing gesture. 'I wouldn't lie to you.'

Sara pressed her palms together. 'I—I think—I think you just like—teasing me——'

'Teasing you?' A look of wry amusement twisted his features. 'Oh, Sara! You're so—inexperienced, aren't you? Do you really think I'm enjoying this?'

Sara shifted her weight from one foot to the other. 'I think I'd better go back to my writing,' she murmured uneasily, but even as she formulated the words he stepped past her, pressing the door firmly closed and leaning back against it.

Her expression must have given her away, because his mouth assumed an impatient slant. 'Don't be alarmed,' he said, straightening. 'I'm not going to satisfy my baser instincts. But Mrs Penworthy is no more expert than you are at playing peeping Tom!'

'You mean——' Sara's voice was scarcely more than a whisper as she gestured disbelievingly towards the door, and he nodded.

'Does it surprise you? It shouldn't. The way we live here is a source of curiosity to the whole village, I believe.'

Sara moved her head helplessly, not knowing how to answer him, and as she stood there, trying to dismiss what he had said, he came to stand in front of her. At once his nearness initiated a backward step, but this time his fingers closed around her wrist, and the pressure he exerted prevented her from moving away from him.

'You said——' she began indignantly, and his eyebrows arched provocatively.

'What?'

'—that—that you—wouldn't——'

'Wouldn't what?' There was a certain line of cruelty about his mouth as he looked down at her. 'Touch you? Ah, but didn't I also say that you were inexperienced? And innocent?' His lower lip protruded. 'To that I'll add—susceptible.'

'You swine!' Sara gazed up at him helplessly, still aware that Mrs Penworthy might be outside the door listening and not wanting to incite any more gossip, and his lips twitched in reluctant sympathy.

'Yes, I am, aren't I?' he agreed, imprisoning both her wrists with one of his, and stroking her instantly averted cheek with the other. 'But then a man in my position has to take his chances when they're offered.'

With her heart pounding madly in her ears, Sara wondered how much of this she could honestly take, before something irrevocable happened. For so long her mother had protected her against any kind of raw emotion, but when Michael was close to her as he was now, there was no way on earth she could fight the excitement he was arousing. Nor did she want to, truthfully; only common sense and the need for self-preservation forced her to make the effort.

Her futile struggles were to no avail. Almost in slow motion, his hand moved to the collar of her shirt, loosening the buttons at the neckline and exposing the fluttering pulse he could see beating there.

'Why are you frightened of me?' he demanded huskily, bending his head to touch that revealing pulse with his tongue. 'Mmm, so much energy expended for so little. Hasn't anyone ever told you that such defencelessness incites the brute in a man?'

'You—you would know about that better than me,' she got out jerkily, and he made a sound of impatience.

'Stop fighting me,' he commanded, finding the fastening of her waistcoat and separating it easily. 'I'm not going to hurt you, so why not enjoy it?'

'Think of England, you mean?' she spat, gazing up at him angrily, and his eyes mirrored his aggravation.

'Why do you persist in doing this?' he exhorted, staring down at her frustratedly. 'You may be inexperienced, but I'm not, and I know you want me as much as I want you!'

Sara gasped. 'I do not! Women—women are not like men——'

'Some women aren't, I know. But you're not one of them.'

'What do you mean?'

For a moment he did not reply, and her tautness and apprehension became almost unbearable. Then, allowing a careless finger to stroke an imaginary line from just below her ear, across her throat to the dusky hollow between her breasts, he said:

'Some women don't enjoy sex. Some women would like to, but can't. You,' his eyes softened sensuously, 'you're not like them.'

Her face blazed. 'Don't talk like that!'

'Why not?'

'Because ...' All her childish inhibitions came back to her. 'Because—it's not right.'

'Why isn't it right?' He was annoyingly persistent. 'What have you been taught? That one shouldn't discuss these things?'

'Yes!'

'Why? Isn't it better to be honest with one another?'

'Honest?' She gulped. 'I wouldn't call it that.' She summoned all her small store of confidence, and continued: 'You—you know you wouldn't talk that way to—to anyone else——'

'True.'

'—only to me. Because—because you think I'm gullible.'

'I've never said that.'

'You said I was susceptible,' she accused, and he nodded.

'You are. Particularly to your emotions.' He allowed his roving finger to probe further, finding the rounded swell of her breasts, the hardening nipples that responded eagerly to his caress. His voice thickened. 'You don't really object to me touching you, Sara,' he muttered, looking down at the result of his explorations. 'Your body gives you away. So why don't you kiss me, and stop wasting so much time!'

Although Sara moved her head urgently from side

to side, his mouth found hers with unerring accuracy. However, his hand holding both of hers was between them, preventing a closer embrace, and she pressed her lips together tightly, determined not to prove his theory. She guessed he would not set her free while she continued to fight him, and in spite of the suffocating pressure of his lips she had to remain unresponsive.

She heard his indrawn frustration, felt the increasing hardness of his mouth, and his fingers at her nape digging almost cruelly into her skin. The hand imprisoning hers tightened its grip also, and as he forced her nearer to him her thumbs dug into the hard muscles of his thigh.

It was almost her undoing. As she felt those taut muscles against her fingers, all desire to resist went out of her, but even as her lips softened, he tore his mouth away from hers.

'Why?' he snapped savagely. 'What's wrong with you?'

'I—why——'

'Did pretending to be Diane give you some kind of kick, or something?' he demanded. 'God! I've known some women in my time, but not one of them was like you!'

Sara was trembling, but his words about Diane had dispelled her momentary weakness. It was a horrible thing to suggest, and she was disgusted. How dared he suggest she was some kind of pervert, only able to respond under certain stimulation?

'You can't believe you don't attract me, can you?' she got out, equally savagely. 'You're so sure of yourself that you actually believe you're irresistible! Well, let me tell you——'

'Don't bother!' His lips twisting bitterly, he brushed

past her and opened the door. 'Go and write your stories! Go and live in that imaginary world you've created for yourself! Because, sure as hell, you're not a part of this one!'

She turned, not prepared to let him have the last word, but he had gone, striding across the hall and presently she heard the front door slam behind him. He had walked out on her once more, and all her resentment and indignation gave way to the most ridiculous desire to burst into tears.

'Will you have your coffee now, miss?'

Even Mrs Penworthy's voice right behind her did not startle her, though it did initiate the speculation as to where the housekeeper had been during her exchange with Michael. Turning, she realised belatedly that her shirt was still halfway unbuttoned, her waistcoat hanging loosely on her shoulders, and that Mrs Penworthy was hardly likely to miss the fact.

Running a hand inside the collar of her shirt, she said: 'I'll have my coffee in the study, if I may, Mrs Penworthy. It—er—it's rather stuffy in the library.'

She didn't know if Mrs Penworthy believed her. In her position, she thought she would probably have had her doubts. But she had successfully spiked any question as to why she should have unfastened her shirt.

In the study, however, she left the coffee untouched, rummaging in her handbag for her medication. Weariness, like a wave of lethargy, was sweeping over her, and as she dissolved the tablet under her tongue she felt a deepening sense of despair. Every time she was with Michael, every time he touched her or kissed her, the feelings of resentment at her weakness increased, and right now she felt a sense of self-disgust that was almost suicidal.

Realising there was no point in trying to work in this mood, she waited until Mrs Penworthy had left the house and then emerged from the study. Pacing restlessly from room to room, she tried to find a measure of the self-possession she had always sustained, but it would not come. The sense of weakness had not left her, but her mind was too agitated to allow her to rest, and when she pressed a hand to her heart she could feel its uneven palpitation. She felt sick, and a little dizzy, and she knew the best thing for her to do would be to go to bed, but the idea of lying there, picturing Michael's possible reactions to her rejection, picturing him with another woman, did not bear consideration. He had said she wanted him, and she did, desperately, so desperately in fact that she felt ill with the knowledge that she had denied it.

CHAPTER SEVEN

SHE opened her eyes to find Michael's lean anxious face suspended above her. Convinced she must be dreaming, she lifted her hand, almost tentatively at first, to touch his tanned cheek, and then felt her cold fingers engulfed by the enveloping warmth of his. He moved her hand along his jawline, over the roughening stubble of his beard to his mouth, pressing her palm to his lips with convulsive urgency. His touch aroused sensations that were very far from dreamlike, and she blinked rapidly, realising suddenly she was lying on her bed. But it was daylight outside, and judging by the angle of the sun, not yet too late in the afternoon, and yet when she tried to remember what happened, her mind was a complete blank.

'God!' Michael's harsh ejaculation attracted her attention, and she watched almost detachedly as he strove to control his relief. 'I thought you were never going to come round. Don't ever do that to me again, do you hear? I don't think I could stand it.'

Sara gazed up at him a trifle perplexedly. 'Come round?' she echoed, her earlier sense of wellbeing evaporating a little. 'Did I—did I pass out?'

'You must have done.' Michael removed her hand from his lips, holding it between both of his, unaware of the pressure in his grasp. 'I came in and found you lying in the hall. I thought at first you'd fallen down the stairs, but there isn't a mark on you, and the way you were lying—well, I don't think you fell.'

'No.' Sara had to take his word for it, trying desperately to remember why she should have collapsed. She
seemed to recall having been in the library, but after
that everything was blacked out. 'I—I must have
fainted. I didn't mean to frighten you.'

'Frighten me! *God!*' Michael's eyes were dark and
tormented. 'Sara, when I came in and found you, for
one awful moment I thought you were dead! I don't
know what I'd have done if that had been so. Killed
myself, I think,' he finished flatly.

'Michael!' Sara's eyes widened to startled orbs.
'Don't say things like that.' She extricated her hand
from his and levered herself up on her elbows. 'I'm all
right now, really I am. It—it was nothing, honestly.
Just a faint, that's all. Nothing to get so uptight about.'

Michael stared at her for a long disturbing moment,
and as their eyes met, Sara began to remember why she
had been so upset earlier. Blurred images of herself
and Michael, locked in combat of a different kind,
invaded the outer limits of her consciousness, bringing
with them the memory of feelings, suppressed and dangerous. She began to tremble, and Michael, seeing the
goose-bumps on her skin, smothered an oath.

'You've probably caught your death of cold, lying on
the floor!' he muttered, getting up from the bed and
looking down at her with open concern. 'Perhaps I
ought to call Gwithian. He at least could give you something to check any infection——'

'No!' Sara stretched a hand towards him imploring
him not to continue. 'Michael, you're exaggerating this
out of all proportion. I don't need a doctor. I—I've
probably been overworking, that's all.'

She offered a silent prayer for forgiveness for this
latter statement, but somehow she had to divert him.

She could not have Doctor Gwithian coming here, discovering her secret. Not when she was succeeding so well.

Michael's taut features showed his indecision. He was probably torn between satisfying himself that she was unharmed, and the obvious complications that introducing her to the local doctor would create. Somehow she had to reassure him, and taking a deep breath, she swung her feet to the floor and sat up. Her head swam a little, but that was not unnatural after losing consciousness, and ignoring this evidence of her weakness, she got to her feet.

'Hey!' Michael caught her arm as she swayed, and she was glad of his support, even though he stared at her rather impatiently. 'You don't have to prove your point,' he muttered. 'I can see you look much better already. But you won't, if you don't take it easy.'

Sara couldn't prevent herself from slanting a look up at him. He was showing such concern, and half provocatively she finger-walked up his lapel to touch his neck. 'You looked pretty sick yourself when I opened my eyes,' she murmured. 'As if you'd seen a ghost.'

'I thought I had,' he retorted huskily, and as he removed her fingers from his shoulder she remembered how he had left her.

'You went—out,' she said hesitantly. 'Why did you come back?'

It was Michael who hesitated now, putting her away from him and going around the end of the bed, resting his arms on the curved iron rail. 'Would you believe— to apologise?' he offered at last, and her lips parted in an unbelieving gasp.

'No ...'

'Why not?'

She shook her head helplessly. 'I—why—you were angry when you left here. Furiously angry. I—I don't believe you'd come back to apologise for that.'

'Then you tell me,' he suggested, with narrowing eyes, and she thought what a fool she was to start this over again.

'To—to pack your things, perhaps,' she ventured now, her voice gathering strength as it gathered confidence. 'I—I think you intended to leave. In fact, I'm sure of it. You may have hoped I'd try to stop you, but that was your intention, wasn't it?'

Michael rested his chin on his arm and regarded her through his lashes. 'Very clever,' he complimented her. 'How very astute.' He lifted his head. 'All right, I admit it. Leaving did cross my mind. But I was going to speak to you first.'

'Were you?'

She sounded sceptical, but he inclined his head towards her. 'Of course. I wouldn't have just walked out on you. But it didn't happen that way.'

He stared at her for several more disruptive seconds, and then walked purposefully towards the door. His hand closed on the handle, but before he could open it Sara had taken a couple of steps after him, grasping the bedpost for support, and demanding huskily: 'Where—where are you going now?'

He turned, surveying her broodingly. 'Well, I'm not leaving, if that's what you're concerned about,' he replied tersely. 'But you should rest, and I thought I'd drive into Torleven to get some cigars. I've run out.'

'Take me with you!'

The words were out before she could prevent them, and besides, she didn't want to prevent them. She wanted to go with him. She wanted to *be* with him.

And right now, she didn't much care what he might think.

'Sara ...' He wrenched open the door, as if by destroying the room's intimacy he could destroy the intimacy between them. 'Why do you want to come with me? You—don't even like me.'

'I do, I do.' She took another step towards him, realising as she stepped off the bedside rug that he had removed her boots. 'Michael! Michael, please! Let me come.'

'Sara, Torleven is a matter of two miles, no more!'

'So what? I need some fresh air—Mrs Penworthy said so. *Please!*'

His eyes darkened, and he turned abruptly away. 'I can't stop you ...' he muttered, and went out of the room.

Putting on boots with hasty fingers was a nerve-racking performance. Time after time, she caught the leather in the zip, and she was thoroughly exhausted by the time she had completed the task. Then she had to find her coat, and she stumbled down the stairs some minutes later, half afraid he might have gone without her.

He appeared from the drawing room as she reached the hall, however, his lips tightening impatiently at the dewing of sweat along her brow. 'Don't you have any more sense?' he demanded, glaring at her angrily, and then turned away again when she gave an apologetic shrug.

The car was an elderly Jaguar, old-fashioned in design, but scarcely used. 'Adam's,' he remarked laconically, settling her into the front seat beside his. 'Or Diane's, just as you care to believe.'

Sara's shoulders sagged against the soft upholstery.

She was glad to rest her head back and allow her trembling limbs to relax, but when Michael came to take the seat beside her, his expression revealed he was not unaware of her weariness.

'You're crazy, do you know that?' he demanded, putting the car into gear and turning down the drive. 'Why couldn't you have stayed at the house until I got back? You're not fit to be walking around.'

'But I'm not walking around, am I?' she countered softly, and he muttered an expletive as they reached the coast road.

Torleven was an attractive place on a sunny afternoon. A fishing boat had just come in, and several people were gathered on the quayside, waiting for the catch to be unloaded. Swarms of gulls soared overhead, just waiting for the fish to be gutted, and several cats preaned on the sea wall, licking their whiskers.

A row of small shops fronted the quay, and the streets that ran up from the harbour were narrow and cobblestoned. All the cottages were painted white, which added to the village's air of cleanliness, the tulips and geraniums growing in window-boxes adding vivid splashes of colour.

Michael parked the car outside one of the shops on the quay, and left her to get his cigars. While he was gone, Sara watched the unloading of the fishing boat, and some of the people gathered there turned to stare at her. They probably recognised the car, she guessed wryly, but she was glad when Michael returned and they drove away.

'What's wrong?' he asked, noticing the colour in her cheeks. 'Too much attention? I warned you there was talk about us. And you're too beautiful to be ignored.'

Sara grimaced. 'You're very gallant all of a sudden.'

'No.' He glanced sideways at her. 'Only honest.'
Then he removed one hand from the wheel to cover
her knee. 'Tell you what, how do you fancy driving to
Penzance? We could have a meal there, as it's Mrs Penworthy's night off. I know she's left a cold buffet,' he
added, as she opened her mouth to protest, 'but that
won't take any harm. We can have it for lunch tomorrow.'

Sara looked at him doubtfully. In her haste to accompany him, she had left her handbag at the house,
and she knew·she dared not go all the way to Penzance
without the reassurance of her bottle of tablets.

'I—I can't go anywhere like this,' she said now, conscious of those hard fingers on her leg. 'I mean, I'm
not wearing any make-up!'

'You look all right to me,' he retorted, withdrawing
his hand to change into a lower gear as they climbed
the coast road. 'What do you really mean? That you
don't want to go to Penzance with me?'

'No!' Sara was indignant. 'I—I would like to go with
you——'

'So?'

'—but couldn't we call at the house first? So that I
could—tidy myself.'

'Change your clothes, you mean?' Michael's eyes ap-
praised her. 'Wear something more—feminine?'

Sara sighed. 'If—if you want me to. But I warn you,
I didn't bring an evening dress.'

Michael frowned. 'Do you honestly feel up to this?'

Sara nodded.

'All right. But don't be long. It's after five now, and
it's quite a drive.'

He followed her into the hall of the house, but as
she went towards the study his voice stopped her.

'What are you doing?'

Sara turned. 'My—handbag,' she said, indicating the room behind her. 'I was just going to get it.'

'I'll get that,' declared Michael brusquely. 'You get ready. I'll see you down here in fifteen minutes.'

She had no choice but to accept his offer, but she climbed the stairs with some misgivings. What was she going to wear? She didn't feel like getting changed at all, but somehow she had to make the effort.

The only item of truly feminine attire she had brought with her was a printed silk shirtwaister that was suitable for any occasion. The sleeves were elbow-length and cuffed, and the waistline was drawn in with matching strings, giving a bloused effect. The skirt was full and pleated, and swung against her slender legs, and she managed to find a pair of unladdered tights to wear with high-heeled black sandal-shoes. With her hair combed and silky, and an eye-shadow adding mystery to eyes already darkened with exhaustion, she looked good, and she decided that half her weariness was due to suppressed emotion. Perhaps if she relaxed, if she let her feelings dictate her mood, just for once she might feel as good as she looked.

The sheepskin was the only coat she had brought with her, and she slung it around her shoulders as she went down the stairs. Michael was right, she thought, she did wear too many masculine clothes. It was good to feel completely feminine again.

Michael was in the drawing room when she came downstairs, standing in front of the fire, which Mrs Penworthy had tended before she left. There were oil-heated radiators in the house, but fires were so much more homely, and Sara had been glad of their cosy warmth during the long lonely evenings.

Michael turned as she appeared in the doorway. He, too, had changed, swapping his jeans for a pair of black suede pants, and his corded jacket for a dark blue velvet one. She had never seen him looking more alien or more attractive, and she felt the disturbing tingling of awareness when the sensual twisting of his mouth told her that he found her attractive, too. But then her eyes dropped to what he was holding in his hands, and she had to grasp the door frame for support as he exhibited it between his forefinger and thumb. It was her bottle of tablets, and she remembered too late that she had left them lying on the desk in the study.

'What are these?' he enquired, inexorably, crossing the space between them to hold them in front of her face. '*Pectotone!* What is Pectotone? What's it for? And what are you doing with them?'

Sara drew a deep breath. 'Is it anything to do with you?' she countered, playing for time. Then: 'They're a treatment for—for asthma, if you must know.'

'*Asthma!*' Michael gazed at her. Then he looked at the label on the bottle again. 'Asthma!' he repeated, and for one awful moment she thought he had recognised the drug. 'You have—asthma?'

Sara expelled her breath unevenly. 'I—I'm afraid so.'

'My God!' Michael's relief was palpable, and she despised herself in that minute for lying to him so blatantly. 'And I thought ...' He shook his head. 'I thought you must be some kind of—of addict. I don't know.' He pressed the bottle into her limp hands. 'That explains everything, doesn't it? Lord, I was beginning to think you must have taken an overdose earlier.'

Sara forced a smile. 'I'm not a drug addict,' she assured him faintly, glad at least in this instance she could be honest. 'I—where's my handbag?'

'On the chair there.' Michael made a gesture towards the hearth, but as she would have moved past him he caught her arm. 'I—don't mind, you know,' he muttered huskily, his gaze lingering on her mouth. 'I mean—asthma doesn't scare me, or anything.' He sighed, his gaze shifting lower to the enticing hollow visible below the neckline of her dress. 'That is—if you thought—if you even imagined—that being an asthmatic would make any difference to my feelings for you——'

'Michael, *please*!' This was something she couldn't stand, and with a snarl of impatience he released her, waiting by the door as she collected her handbag from the armchair by the fire.

The drive to Penzance took longer than even Michael had anticipated. The roads were busy with home-going motorists, and as well as local traffic, there were the occasional tourists, towing their caravans, clogging the narrow highways. It was as well Michael had to concentrate on his driving, Sara thought, as they hardly spoke to one another, and she wondered rather hysterically how generously he would react to her real condition. He thought he understood, but he didn't understand at all.

Sara had never been to Penzance before, and she looked with interest at its narrow High Street, with the pavement elevated above the road. She saw the heliport, and the harbour, and restrained her curiosity when Michael turned off the road on to a cobbled track that led up beside an old boathouse. A crown and anchor hanging outside a building just behind the boathouse indicated a public house, but after Michael had parked the Jaguar, and they crossed the tiny car-park to enter the lighted porchway of the inn, she saw it was also a small, but intimate, restaurant.

The head waiter, or perhaps he was the owner, Sara couldn't be sure, recognised her companion and came towards them welcomingly. 'Michael!' he exclaimed, shaking his hand warmly. 'We didn't expect to see you again this week.' His eyes flickered over Sara. 'A table for two, is it?'

'That's right. But we'll have a drink first.' Michael put a hand beneath Sara's elbow, and indicated the bar opposite. 'Dinner in—half an hour, eh, Patrick? We're in no hurry.'

The man made an expansive gesture, and with a brief smile Michael guided Sara into the bar. Once there, his hand fell away, and his face was sombre as he indicated the stools at the bar.

'What will you have?' he asked, taking her coat from her shoulders and folding it on to an adjoining stool. 'A Martini? Sherry? Or something else?'

'A—Martini would be fine,' she answered, glancing about her at the ship's wheel on the wall, and the lanterns hung over the bar. 'This is nice. Do you come here often?'

Michael ordered their drinks, then levered himself on to the stool beside her. The bar was empty at this hour of the evening, and apart from an old man seated in a corner, smoking his pipe, they had the place to themselves.

'A—friend of mine introduced me to it,' Michael remarked shortly, helping himself to some nuts off the bar. 'And it happened that I already knew Patrick Keegan. We were at school together.'

'I see.' Sara cupped her chin on her knuckles, resting her elbow on the bar. 'And is—Mr Keegan—the owner?'

'That's right.'

Michael was curt, and on impulse she turned to him, running tentative fingers over his shoulder. The material of his jacket was sensuously soft to the touch, but the muscle beneath was satisfyingly hard. When he didn't flinch away, she leant closer, resting her chin on her fingers and saying, so that her breath fanned his ear:

'Don't be angry with me, please! Can't we just be friends? I don't want to spoil the evening.'

Michael turned his head to look at her, and she was forced to draw back a little to meet his stare. This close, the irises of his eyes seemed almost golden, their smouldering fire evidence of his simmering mood.

'I am not angry with you,' he declared, though his tone hinted otherwise. 'But I'm only human, Sara, and you're too intelligent a person not to know what's wrong with me.'

Sara's tongue made a provocative appearance, and although she was inclined to withdraw her hand, she did not do so. 'I gather you approve of my dress,' she murmured instead, allowing her fingertips to stroke his ear lobes, and it was he who broke their visual contact, hunching his shoulders as he picked up the glass containing the whisky he had ordered for himself.

Sara was intoxicated by her success. It was the first time in her life she had tested the strength of her own sex appeal, and Michael's reaction had been definitely positive. It made her want to go on, to see how far she could go, and the reassuring surroundings of the bar urged her to try.

'I like your jacket,' she said now, deliberately allowing her fingers to brush the hair at his nape as she stroked his collar. 'It's so soft—so smooth! I like touching it.'

Michael expelled an uneven breath, but he made no response, and encouraged by his restraint, she actually ran her fingers into his hair, tugging them down through the dark silky strands.

'I'd advise you to give it up,' he said suddenly, without looking at her. 'Unless you want more trouble than you expect.' And at her horrified withdrawal, he continued dryly: 'I realise you feel secure here, but don't forget, we go home together.'

Sara took a hasty taste of her own drink, grimacing at the raw flavour of vermouth. But at least it gave her something to do, and with trembling fingers she helped herself to some ice from the barrel on the bar. Michael turned to look at her again as she fumbled with the ice, and as she caught his eye, her features stiffened resentfully. Was he laughing at her? There seemed a definite twitch to his lips, and she pursed hers as she dropped two squares of ice into her drink.

'I do like your dress,' he said suddenly, taking the tongs from her and retaining his hold on her hand. 'And I guess I am a moody devil. But I've never felt this way about a woman before, and I don't honestly know how to handle it.'

He was suddenly so serious, so sincere—and his words seemed to tear her to pieces. 'Michael——' she began, wanting to reassure him, but unable to find the words she wanted to say.

'Oh, what the hell——'

With a muffled oath, he curved a hand round the back of her neck and pulled her mouth to his. He did not seem to care who might be watching them, and after the first few seconds, neither did Sara. Somehow she was off the bar stool and between his legs, conscious of his stirring muscles against her stomach and careless of the incongruity of their surroundings. He was devouring her, she thought fancifully, but she was as eager as he was to satisfy his hungry passion.

She came to her senses to find her face cupped between his hands, and when she reluctantly opened her eyes it was to find Michael watching her with a devastatingly tender expression on his face.

'Why didn't you kiss me like that this afternoon?' he demanded in a low voice, his thumb probing the corner of her mouth. 'I knew I wasn't mistaken about you. You're all fire beneath that cool exterior. And I want you, Sara. I *need* you——'

'*Mike!* Mike, it is you, isn't it? Heavens, I didn't know you were coming here tonight.'

The light feminine voice hailed them from the doorway of the small bar, and Sara scarcely had time to struggle free before the young woman reached them. Michael had not wanted to let her go, and the slumbrous emotion in his eyes gave way to mild impatience as he turned to face the newcomer. Sara was aware of his impatience, and guessed it was with her, but she couldn't help it. She was overwhelmingly conscious of her own dishevelled appearance, and half infuriated that he could appear so cool and composed when only minutes before she had felt his aroused body thrusting against hers.

Maybe he was still aroused, she thought, rather spitefully, as she saw that the girl who had come to join them was a strikingly attractive creature. She was tall, and red-haired, and her voluptuous curves made Sara feel almost boyish in comparison. She was glad she

was not wearing a pants suit, for the other girl was, but
no one, least of all Michael, could have described her
attire as masculine. On the contrary, she was almost
vulgarly feminine, Sara decided, as the other girl's full
breasts swelled against the fastening of her jacket. Who
was she? And what did she want? Could this be one of
the doctor's daughters that Mrs Penworthy had spoken
about?

Michael had greeted the girl warmly, and Sara's lips
tightened as long painted fingernails lingered on his
cheek. He was so casual, she thought angrily, wishing
she knew where the ladies' room was. She didn't want
to meet his girl-friends, and hardly thinking what she
was doing, she picked up her Martini and swallowed
it in a most unfeminine gulp.

'Sara . . .' Michael had turned back to her now, and
she looked at him with guarded eyes.

'Yes?'

'Sara, I want you to meet an old friend of mine—
Marion Morton. Marion, this is Sara Fortune. You remember? She's staying with me at Raven's Mill for a
couple of weeks.'

Sara could have strangled him there and then. Apart
from the unpalatable information that this must be the
Mrs Morton with whom he had been spending so much
of his time, she was appalled that he dared describe
her presence at the house in such ambiguous terms.
She could well imagine what Marion Morton must be
thinking, and her face burned with angry resentment.

'I think you ought to have explained that I didn't
know you were staying in the house when I came to
Ravens Mill!' she retorted now, ignoring the censure
in Michael's eyes. She paused, aware of the embarrassed
silence she had created, and then went on: 'I wonder,

Mrs Morton, could you tell me where the ladies' room is? I'd like to—er—wash my hands.'

'Oh—oh, of course.' Marion exchanged a look with Michael, and then took Sara's arm and drew her to the door, pointing down the passage towards the back of the building. 'It's through there,' she said, her smile irritating Sara even more. 'Can you find it?'

'I should think so,' declared Sara shortly, marching away, aware as she did so that she had never behaved so badly in her life.

Fortunately the tiny cloakroom was empty, and Sara viewed her reflection with horrified eyes. Her lips were bare, and the skin around them had been reddened by the bruising pressure of Michael's mouth. Her cheeks were flushed with hectic colour, and her hair was tangled where his hands had run through it. She looked—*ravaged*; yes, that was the word, she thought in dismay, realising how foolish she must have sounded when she denied any relationship with Michael.

A powder-based make-up erased much of the unsightly chafing, and a brick-coloured lip-gloss gave her mouth a dusky radiance. With her hair combed and silky, and some perfume behind her ears, she felt a little more capable of facing whatever was to come.

Her hopes that Marion Morton might have disappeared in her absence were not realised. The older girl was now seated on one of the stools at the bar, with Michael on one side, and another man on the other. Sara hesitated in the doorway, feeling an intruder. But she was obliged to join them, and she crossed the stone-flagged floor towards them feeling a little of the faintness she had experienced earlier in the day.

Both men got off their stools at her approach, and her eyes went automatically to Michael's. But he avoided her gaze, waiting until she was seated before indicating the other man, and saying: 'This is Norman Morton, Sara—Marion's husband.'

Sara managed to make a polite response to Norman Morton's greeting, but she felt somewhat chastened by his appearance. Obviously he also knew and liked Michael, and her earlier reactions seemed petty and childlike. Of course, it was still possible that Michael's relationship with his boyhood friend was not as innocent as it appeared, but in any case, it was nothing to do with her, and she should not have behaved as she had.

Norman Morton was a mild-mannered Cornishman, tall and dark, broader than Michael, but inclined to soft speaking. When his wife and Michael started talking about horses, he asked Sara about London, and she found herself relaxing in his company and liking his quiet courtesy. She accepted another drink and swallowed it rashly, realising after she had done so that she was not accustomed to drinking at all, but using it as a barrier to the frequently brooding glances Michael cast in her direction.

It was no surprise when Michael suggested they all ate dinner together, and a table for four was quickly provided. Patrick Keegan served them himself, and it was obvious from their conversation that the Mortons were as well acquainted with him as Michael.

'Michael tells me you're writing a book, Sara,' Marion remarked at one point, and Sara forced herself to be polite.

'That's right,' she agreed stiffly. 'It's just a novel for children, though.'

'*Just!*' Marion was impressed. 'I have trouble keeping my ledgers up to date.' She smiled. 'I wouldn't know how to start writing a book!'

'Sara works in a publisher's office,' put in Michael

dauntingly. 'She's used to working with manuscripts.'

'Even so . . .'

Marion was endearingly honest, and Sara was finding it increasingly difficult not to like her. It was not
really her nature to take sudden aversions to people,
and she wished Michael would stop looking at her in
that disagreeable way. She guessed he would not forgive her easily, and she dreaded his hostility on the
journey home.

Because of this, she drank more wine than she was
accustomed to, and by the end of the evening she didn't
much care what he thought of her. Or so she told herself. She felt pleasantly mellow, but she couldn't help
swaying a little when they came out of the inn and the
cool night air hit her.

The Mortons said goodnight and went to find their
own car, and Michael regarded Sara with distant eyes.
'Can you make it?' he asked, and the tone of resigned
toleration in his voice made her feel like a silly schoolgirl. It was as if he was determined to be polite at all
costs, as if behaving as though she didn't know better
cooled his temper. But she would rather have had his
anger after the way she had acted.

Without answering him, she wove her way across the
car-park to where the Jaguar was parked, and with a
shrug of indifference, he unlocked the doors.

'Get in,' he advised, his voice a little harder now, and
with some difficulty, she gathered herself and her skirts
into the squab seat. Then she waited tautly while he
circled the car and got in beside her.

The Mortons' Range Rover was behind them as they
left Penzance, its headlights illuminating the inside of
the Jaguar, making Sara feel a little like a performer in
the spotlight. Still, their searching presence seemed to

restrain Michael from making the outburst she had expected, or perhaps she was wrong, and he had decided
she was not worthy of his contempt.

In consequence, she was obliged to look at the road
ahead, until the constant stream of headlights caused
her eyes to droop and finally to close. She did not know
at what point the Mortons left them, or indeed recall
much of the journey back to Ravens Mill. She opened
her eyes to find the car's engine extinguished, and only
the muted thunder of the ocean disturbing the stillness.

She jerked upright abruptly, looking round for
Michael, but she was alone in the car. Immediately, a
sense of injustice gripped her, that he should leave her
here, to the mercy of any intruder who might enter the
grounds. The fact that it was unlikely that anyone
should wander the grounds of Ravens Mill at this time
of night was immaterial. He had done it, and if the keys
had been in the ignition she would have driven straight
back to London, she thought resentfully.

Sniffing, she reached for her handbag, and as she did
so the door at her side of the car was opened. Shocked,
she gazed into Michael's impatient face with startled
eyes, and his mouth turned down at the corners when
he saw her expression.

'You're awake,' he remarked flatly. 'You seemed dead
to the world when I left you.'

Sara gathered herself with difficulty. 'Is that an
opinion—or an invocation?' she enquired tartly. 'I
probably should be if I was left to sleep out here all
night.'

Michael's mouth tightened. 'As it happens I've been
unlocking the doors, preparatory to carrying you up to
your room,' he told her, with cold emphasis. 'However,
as you seem fit enough to spit at me, you can make your

own way upstairs!'

He walked back towards the lighted entrance, and once again, Sara felt terrible. She should have known he would never have abandoned her. It simply wasn't his nature. And if nothing else, she had learned he had sympathy and compassion.

With a feeling of dejection she got out of the car, closed the door, and walked slowly into the house. There were lights on the stairs, and a light in the library, and without any hesitation she halted by the open door. Michael was pouring himself a brandy when she cleared her throat to attract his attention, but his glance behind was barely cursory, and accompanied by an interrogative lifting of his eyebrows.

'I'm sorry,' she said. 'I'm sorry for—well, for speaking to you as I did just now, and for being rude to— to Mrs Morton.'

There was silence for a few more seconds while Michael lifted the glass he was holding to his lips and swallowed a mouthful of the spirit. When he turned, still holding the glass, she stiffened, but all he said was: 'That's all right then, isn't it?'

'Is it?' Sara was uncertain. She didn't care for the expression in his tawny eyes. She didn't care for the way he was regarding her—as if she was some recalcitrant child, and he was determined to humour her. 'Do you—do you accept my apology?'

'Yes.'

'You don't sound as if you do.'

'I'm sorry.'

Sara pursed her lips. 'That's a meaningless phrase!'

'Yes, isn't it?'

His contempt was belittling as she took his meaning. She could see no glimmer of sympathy or compassion in his eyes at the moment and the glass of brandy in his hand seemed to signify his intention of finding a different kind of satisfaction. But still she had to have one more try.

'I don't know what came over me,' she persisted, running her hands inside the cuffs of her coat. 'I'm not normally so—so——'

'Forget it!'

'How can I?'

'Quite easily, I should think.' Long lashes came to veil his eyes. 'You seem to forget things with remarkable ease, when it suits you.'

Sara clenched her fists. 'Is that supposed to mean something?'

His eyes flickered for a moment, then he shook his head almost wearily. 'No.' He sighed. 'No, go to bed. I'll see you in the morning.'

CHAPTER EIGHT

SLEEP was a long time in coming. Sara tossed and turned for hours, plagued by feelings of guilt and re-crimination, aware that staying here was rapidly be-coming an untenable proposition. During the day, she could fool herself into thinking that she could handle the situation, but lying in the darkness, she could no longer deny that she was playing with emotions too powerful to control. And she had to control them. She loved Michael, that much was obvious, but she could never tell him. Somehow she had to summon the strength to leave here, before she succumbed com-pletely to a wholly unrealistic desire to accept what-ever he was prepared to offer.

How Diane would laugh if she knew what she had done. Selfish, uncaring Diana, who had sent her down here under false pretences, prepared to sacrifice any-one to her own ambition, so long as it wasn't herself. Had she no thought to the consequences? Why hadn't she phoned or written, to find out what was going on? Or had she believed it might all be a bluff, and by con-tacting Sara known she might only be arousing un-necessary suspicions?

With thoughts like these for company, Sara found the escape to oblivion almost impossible to achieve. Even the idea of leaving in the morning evoked a pain, whose physical manifestation was only a vague discomfort compared to its spiritual counterpart. Michael's reactions to her explanation about her tablets came to taunt her, and it was impossible not to carry the thought on from there to its inevitable conclusion. He had said asthma did not scare him, but how might he react if he discovered she was only half a woman, an invalid, like his father's wife, of whom he spoke with a certain amount of disparagement?

She eventually fell into a fitful doze, awakening soon after seven to the chattering chorus of the birds. Any further sleep was impossible, in spite of the comfort of her bed and the earliness of the hour, and she decided to go downstairs and make herself a cup of tea before Mrs Penworthy arrived to prepare breakfast.

The kitchen was chilly, but the kettle soon boiled, and she leant against the draining board while it brewed, staring out at the neglected garden. A few late daffodils struggled between the roots of an ancient elm tree, and the hedges were rapidly losing their skeletal appearance. Soon the blossom would be out along the lanes, and the whole panoply of summer would colour this small corner of Cornwall. Even the ocean would adopt a less threatening appearance, although the rocks below Ravens Mill could never look anything less than treacherous. But she guessed it was possible to swim from the cove, and she envied Michael his ability to climb the cliffs without effort. Of course, Michael might not be here come summer. His home was in Portugal now, he had said so, and perhaps his great-aunt would arrange a marriage for him as her parents had for his grandfather.

The unpleasant trend of her thoughts brought a return of the black feelings of the night before. Forcing them aside, she turned from the window and poured her tea, almost relieved when the scalding liquid splashed her fingers and she had a purely physical pain to contend with. Picking up her cup, she carried it across the kitchen and into the hall, gathering up the skirt of her dressing gown as she climbed the stairs.

She had to pass Michael's room on the way to her own, however, and almost involuntarily she hesitated outside the door. He might like a cup of tea, she told herself, trying to justify her reasons for stopping, but she knew that was not why she wanted so urgently to see him. He would be asleep, and that was why she had this almost compulsive urge to open his door, to look on him unobserved and without embarrassment.

With the teacup still in her hand, she turned the handle and allowed the heavy door to swing inwards. She knew the room, of course. It was where she had slept that first night, that fatal first night.

The room was shadowy, even though the sun was doing its best to force its way between the cracks in the curtains, but Sara saw at once that Michael was still asleep. He was lying on his back, arms stretched above his head, the fine covering of dark hair on his chest arrowing down to his naval. The covers concealed his lower limbs, but she had no doubt that he was naked, and her pulses quickened in concert with her racing blood. If only, she thought, taking a tentative step nearer, her eyes moving down over the muscular outline of his legs, if only ...

'To what do I owe the honour of this visit?'

Michael's brusque tones brought her head up in alarm, and the cup shook perilously in its saucer. Unknown to her, his eyes had opened, and now he was gazing at her with only lightly concealed hostility.

'Oh, I——' She sought around for a suitable excuse, and her trembling fingers drew her attention to the cup she was holding. 'I—I've brought you—some tea!'

'Tea!' He sat bolt upright, uncaring that by doing so the sheets dropped precariously lower. 'Why should you bring me tea?'

Sara swallowed with difficulty. 'I—why else should I come into your room at this hour of the morning?' she countered, glancing behind her. The door was still reassuringly ajar and a little of her confidence returned. 'Would you—would you like a cup?'

Michael's lips twisted. 'All right. Why not? If that's all you're offering me.'

Licking her dry lips, she was forced to move forward, holding the cup out in front of her like some defensive shield. If only he would lean towards her and take it. Then she wouldn't have to go near the bed. But he didn't. He waited until she was actually beside the bed before taking it from her unresisting fingers.

He watched her as he raised the cup to his lips, but she didn't immediately draw away, even though she realised that she could. Now that he had made no move to touch her, she felt curiously let down, and she waited until he tasted the tea, frowning at the grimace he pulled when it was not to his liking.

'This isn't sweetened,' he observed, returning the cup to its saucer. 'Are you sure it's really for me? I thought you would have learned by now that I like things sweet.'

Sara faltered. 'I—er—I——' she started awkwardly, and his eyes glinted sardonically.

'Don't tell me you're sorry again,' he mocked. 'Not after last night!' He surveyed her lazily as he set the cup down on the bedside table. 'No. You thought I'd be asleep. So what brought you in here, I wonder? Curiosity? Surely you know I have no secrets from you!'

Sara's cheeks flamed and she took an involuntary backward step. 'I—I brought the tea,' she insisted, dragging her eyes away from his lean, supple body. 'If—if it's of no use, I'll take it away again.'

'Will you?'

'Yes.' She hesitated. Then, with difficulty: 'Michael, I—I hope your friends didn't think I was too—well, too silly last night. I mean—I thought—that is, I didn't know—what your relationship with Mrs Morton—was.'

The amber eyes darkened as they rested on her half averted face. 'Does it matter?'

'Well, yes. Yes, I think it does. I mean, you were—you were kissing me, and—and I felt—I felt——'

'Embarrassed?'

'No! *Ashamed!*' She met his eyes then with uneasy defiance. 'After all, we only met a week ago——'

'Met?' He uttered a short laugh. 'Well, I suppose that's one way of putting it.'

'Don't make fun of me!' she flared. 'You know what I mean.'

'Yes, I know,' he confirmed brusquely, shocking her by sliding his legs out of bed and getting to his feet. Ignoring her swift intake of breath, he reached for his bathrobe and pulled it on, turning to face her as he tied the cord, his expression far from encouraging. 'What do you have to say, Sara? I suppose last night proved we can't go on in this way. I can't, anyway. I guess the time has come to go to London and let Diane know she's a widow. Not a wealthy one, but comfortable enough. That will please her, no doubt. Me— I'm going back to Coimbra.'

Sara's lips parted in dismay. Lying in bed, going over the possibilities that faced her, leaving had seemed the only answer. By getting away from Ravens Mill, by returning to her life in London, she had thought she might find peace. Yet now, confronted by such an inevitability, she felt only doubt and uncertainty, and the indisputable awareness of her feelings for this man. It was crazy, *madness*, but how could she let him go, not knowing if she would ever see him again?

'I—I suppose there's some girl—some girl in Portugal, who'll be—only too happy to have your baby,' she said on impulse, and he looked at her through narrowed eyes.

'You say the craziest things, do you know that?' he responded at last, a certain hardening around his lips his only apparent reaction. 'Why should you be interested in some mythical girl in Portugal? As a matter of fact, I have a second cousin who would fit the bill admirably. Does that satisfy you?'

'Oh——' Sara's lips trembled. 'Oh, Michael!' She shook her head helplessly, unable to deny the tears that were welling in her eyes. 'And—and what if I said I didn't want you to go? Would—would that be crazy, too?'

A flicker of some uncontrollable emotion burned in the depths of his eyes, but he made no move to touch her, and her hands went out towards him almost in supplication. They gripped the lapels of his bathrobe, moving tentatively over the rough towelling, her fingernails brushing the taut skin of his chest. And all the while her eyes were held by his, riveted by the smouldering golden intensity of his gaze.

'Michael ...' she said again, moving closer, fighting the weakening despair that he might humiliate her further. 'Michael, please, I want you to stay.'

'Sara ...' His voice had thickened in spite of his control. 'Sara, this is not the place to have a conversation like this.'

'Why not?' She moved closer, and as she did so, she could feel the taut muscles of his thighs. 'Michael, there's still a few days of my holiday left. Couldn't we—make a fresh start?'

'Dear God!' His hands went up to grip her wrists. 'Sara! Sara, you don't know what you're asking. I—I'm only human, not some kind of machine. Living with you—living in the same house as you, is driving me crazy, do you know that? I don't know what it is about you, but you've got under my skin, and I can't take much more of this—this *friendship* you want.'

'How do you know what I want?' she breathed recklessly, and heard the harsh imprecation he uttered.

'Don't say that, Sara! Don't fool me! You're not the kind of girl to become any man's mistress. And I don't want you that way. I don't know what you want, but don't play with me.'

'Oh, Michael ...' Her tongue appeared with provocative brevity. Even like this, holding her away from him, she could sense his arousal, could smell the musky male scent of his body. She had never known she could feel this way about a man, not only loving him, but wanting him, too. There was a disturbing ache in her lower limbs, and she longed to feel the hungry passion of his mouth, the searching intimacy of his hands, the fulfilling satisfaction only his possession could give ... 'Michael, love me ...'

'God help me, I do!' he swore angrily, and this time she had no complaint about his responses. His admission was against her mouth, and when her lips moved against his, his words gave way to a low groan of satisfaction.

Sara's senses swam beneath the eager hunger of his lips. Close against the hard muscles of his chest, her breasts swelled and grew taut, surging against the cotton of her nightgown. Michael's fingers pushed her dressing gown from her shoulders, and then found the straps of her nightgown, shedding it as well.

'Beautiful ...' he muttered, swinging her up into his arms, and Sara had no thought for anything but him and the physical expression of their love ...

She made only one half-hearted murmur that Mrs Penworthy would be arriving shortly, but Michael was in no fit state to consider that possibility in any serious way.

'To hell with Mrs Penworthy,' he said, lowering her to the tumbled covers, and looking down at her with disturbed and disturbing eyes. 'You're all I care about. All I'll ever want ...'

She did not know what she had expected, but certainly nothing like the pleasure that spread over her and around her, wrapping her in a warm feeling of lethargy and fulfilment. There had been pain, but she had been prepared for that, and what came after was so much more than she had ever imagined. Michael had been so patient with her, so gentle, so tender that she had responded to him without inhibition, giving and sharing, and learning how to please him as well as herself.

Afterwards, Michael lay on his side looking down at her with undisguised satisfaction, and now she felt no embarrassment, only an intense awareness of the poignancy of the situation.

'Loving,' he said, bending his head to touch her parted lips with his own. 'Making love. I never knew the meaning of the word until now.'

Sara's heart was not immune to statements of that kind, but the knowledge that somehow she had cheated him was tugging at her. What did he expect of her now? What could she give? When she had so little to offer?

'I love you,' he added, rubbing his tongue against one pink-tipped nipple, and her body was still not proof against that tantalising arousal. 'You taste delicious, you know,' he continued, his hands conducting their own exploration. 'Soft, and smooth, and inexpressibly sweet!'

'Oh, Michael . . .'

'Don't talk,' he commanded softly, his mouth moving up to her mouth, and beneath its searching pressure she had no will to deny him.

When he at last released her lips she was breathless, and there was a curiously possessive smugness in his disruptive gaze. 'You do love me,' he muttered, as if he only just believed it. 'Oh, Sara, when will you marry me?'

'Michael—Michael——'

'Would someone like to tell me exactly what is going on here?'

The stridently feminine tones were totally unexpected. Mrs Penworthy would never have dared to interrupt them in quite that way, but Sara was so drugged with the aftermath of their lovemaking that not even the sight of Diane Tregower, glaring at them from the open doorway, could inspire more than a disbelieving drawing-together of her eyebrows. Shock and reaction would come later, but now all she was concerned with was pulling the bed-covers protectively about them.

Michael's reactions were much less obvious. Turning on to his back, he surveyed Diane with narrowed,
calculating eyes, and his response to her question was
as cool as hers had been heated.

'You must be Diane!' he observed, without concern.
'I thought you would turn up sooner or later.'

Sara's hands trembled as she drew the brush through
the long silky length of her hair. She was trying to
hurry, but her nerves would not let her, and although
she kept telling herself that she had nothing to fear,
the words had a hollow ring. Why had she chosen to
wear the velvet pants suit? she wondered, regarding her
reflection with something akin to dislike. Diane was
always so elegant, so *feminine*; why hadn't she worn
a skirt or a dress, anything to reinforce her failing
confidence? It was too late now to change again, but in
any case she could not compete with Diane, not on
those levels. Instead she turned her mind to the confrontation ahead of her, and wished that somehow she
might escape it. If only she could run away, *hide*, do
anything which might relieve her of the necessity of
facing Diane so soon after what had happened.

Putting down the brush, she leant closer to the
mirror to brush an imaginary eyelash from her cheek.
Her cheeks were not pale at the moment; they were
warm and flushed with colour, accentuating the limpid
clarity of her eyes. There was a fullness to her mouth
which had not been there before, and no matter how
she tried, she could not erase the unmistakable languor
of Michael's lovemaking.

Michael ...

Her heart skipped a beat. Just thinking of him, of
what he had done, brought a stirring awareness of how

vulnerable she was. It had not been easy deceiving him, yet she had done it. But now Diane was here, and she could destroy her carefully-contrived illusion with just a careless word.

She moistened her dry lips. Of course, it had been a shock for Diane, too. Sara knew her so well, and she knew when the colour flared into the other girl's face that Diane was having difficulty in holding on to her temper. It must have been a revelation, after all. Sara—quiet, unassuming, *delicate* Sara—sleepy-eyed and cat-content, after the kind of interlude Diane would never have expected her to experience. Cool, studious Sara, with her love of books and writing, avoiding all emotional entanglements, able to be manipulated, in spite of the latent weaknesses of her condition. Diane had always treated her with a certain amount of contempt, she realised that now, and finding her in bed with the kind of man Diane always found most attractive, must have shaken her to the core of her being.

Drawing an unsteady breath, Sara straightened and surveyed herself once more. Diane was downstairs now, waiting for her to dress and join her. Michael was supposedly dressing, too, although he seemed infinitely less concerned about his sister-in-law's appearance than she did. Of course, he did not know she had any reason to fear Diane, or more accurately, what she *knew* about Sara, and he had seemed to find her anger amusing. Unlike that other occasion, when he had allowed Sara to escape him as soon as Marion Morton appeared, he had forcibly prevented her from getting out of bed, holding her against him, and taunting Diane with the evident intimacy of their relationship.

Diane had been furious—Sara had known that. But instead of demanding to know who Michael was, or what he was doing here, she had turned on her heel and left them, throwing the words that she would speak to Sara downstairs back over her shoulder.

Sara shivered now, in spite of the fact that outside the sun was making its presence felt. She didn't know why Diane had come here, or what her intention was, but she was experienced enough to realise that having angered her, her position was that much less secure. Diane did not take kindly to being embarrassed or humiliated, and Michael had done both.

As if thinking of him had conjured his image, the door behind her suddenly opened, and he appeared. Like herself, Michael had dressed. He was wearing similar clothes to her own—tight-fitting black pants, a loose-sleeved white shirt, and a black waistcoat. But whereas she had hesitated over their suitability, there was no doubt that they accentuated his maleness. With his dark hair smoothly combed, and the shadow of beard shaved from his jawline, he looked much different from the lover who had tumbled her on his bed, and yet, when she looked into his eyes, they held exactly the same question.

He came into her bedroom and closed the door, and immediately she panicked. 'I—why—we ought to be going downstairs,' she began anxiously. 'I mean— Diane will be wondering what we're doing, and as I don't know why—why she's here——'

Michael used a word before Diane's name that Sara had never actually heard spoken before. But its meaning was unmistakable, as he continued: '*I* know why she's here!' And as Sara digested this, he added: 'I sent for her. Yesterday. When you thought I went to buy some cigars!'

'You—sent—for—her!' Sara stared at him disbeliev-

ingly. Then she shook her head, as if to clear the fuzzi-
ness of her brain. 'You sent for her?' she repeated
blankly. 'But—why? *How?*'

Michael thrust his thumbs into the waistband of his
pants, his expression mirroring his own self-disgust.
'I—I was worried about you,' he muttered. 'You
seemed—oh *God*!' He raked back his hair impatiently.
'How was I to know—do you think, if I'd thought——'
He broke off and came towards her, and although she
backed away, her thighs came up against the edge of
the dressing table. 'Hey . . .' he muttered, his hands curv-
ing over her shoulders. 'Don't look at me like that. You
frightened me yesterday. I guess . . .' He looked down at
her tenderly. 'I guess I thought I was to blame for—
well, for the blackouts. It wasn't until you told me—
when I found those pills——'

'Michael, *please*——'

She found she couldn't bear to listen to him, knowing she had lied to him all along. She wanted to tell
him the truth, oh *God*! how she wanted to tell him
the truth. But the words simply wouldn't come.

'Sara . . .' His voice had thickened perceptibly, and
he swore softly under his breath. 'Sara, we have to get
things straight between us, before we get involved with
that bitch downstairs. I love you. I think you know that
now, don't you? And I believe you love me. Say you'll
marry me. Please! Don't let Diane foul this up for
us. Remember, she sent you down here. Remember
what she did to Adam. Don't let her corrupt your feelings by persuading you I'm any more of an unprin-
cipled swine than I already feel!'

'Michael . . .' Sara caught her lower lip between her
teeth. 'Michael, you don't know what you're saying.'

'I do.' The hands on her shoulders tightened, and

the lines that bracketed his mouth became a little more pronounced. 'Sara, what do I have to do to persuade you? I'm not a poor man, if that's what you're thinking. I may not be a wealthy one either, but we won't starve. And if you don't want to live in Portugal, then I'll find a job in England.' His eyes softened as they rested on her parted lips. 'You know, Dona Isabella is going to love you.'

'Michael, no! No! I can't marry you!'

'What do you mean?'

His face was paler under his tan, and somehow she managed to free herself from his grasp. He was staring at her as if he couldn't believe what he had just heard, yet beneath the mask of pain that contorted his features, there was a dawning bitterness that brought a grim twist to his mouth.

'I see,' he said now, between clenched teeth. 'I'm not good enough for you, is that it? The by-blow of an over-sexed landlord and a gipsy! Oh, yes, I understand. You wanted a sexual experience, and I supplied it, is that it? My, my, that cool exterior of your does hide a multitude of contradictions, doesn't it? Perhaps I've misjudged Diane. At least she doesn't attempt to hide the faults in her character. She's honest about her failings. She doesn't pretend emotions she's incapable of really feeling!'

'Nor do I!' Sara caught her breath, unable to deny the instinctive retort. 'Michael, it's not that I don't—that is—it has nothing to do with—with you, with your parentage or your prospects. Oh, God! I—just—don't want to marry—anyone!'

Michael's expression mirrored the scorn he felt for her futile protestations. 'There's someone else, isn't there?' he snapped. 'This—man you came away to for-

get. It's him, isn't it? You're still in love with him!
What will you do now? Go back to him, in spite of
his apparent shortcomings? Was he married? Was that
it? And couldn't you take the chance of going to bed
with him, in case you got pregnant? Well, how do you
feel now? Secure? Experienced? Or simply reckless?'

'I tell you, it's not like that!' Sara was desperate
now. 'Michael, there is no one else.'

'No?' Clearly he didn't believe her. 'Well, no matter.
For some reason best known to yourself, you've turned
me down. Perhaps I'll have better luck with Diane.'

'What do you mean?' Sara paled perceptibly, and he
sneered.

'Why not? I don't think she'll object. I got the distinct impression that your *alter ego* would not be
averse to taking your place!'

'Oh!' Sara was shocked now. 'Oh, you wouldn't.
You—you *couldn't*!'

'Couldn't I?' He shrugged. 'We'll see.'

Sara gulped, a sickly nausea sweeping over her as
she stared into his unrelenting features. 'You—you—
I—I——'

'—hate me?' he supplied coldly, and she turned
her head helplessly from side to side.

'You—you say you love me, and then—and then——'

'Jealous?' he queried, but beneath the mockery there
was an underlying note of intensity in his voice that she
desperately wanted to respond to. Instead she shook
her head again, turning away, a feeling of complete
impotence threatening to engulf her.

She heard the door slam behind her, and only then
did she turn to look after him, fighting back the tears
that burned behind her eyes. But what else could she
do? She asked herself despairingly. She could never

put him in the position of feeling obligated to honour the commitment he had proposed. Better to be despised than pitied.

Realising she could delay no longer, she cast a final look at her reflection before walking towards the door. Right now, she had Diane to face, and she would need all her strength to combat the kind of malice the other girl was likely to display.

Downstairs, she hesitated before making her way to the dining room. The sound of Mrs Penworthy's voice was reassuring, and she paused for a moment in the doorway, wondering what that lady was making of this sudden change in the situation.

Michael and Diane were seated opposite one another, and the housekeeper was in the process of setting a pot of coffee beside Diane's plate. They all looked up when Sara appeared, and after only a momentary hesitation, Michael rose politely to his feet.

'Oh ...' Sara was embarrassed. 'Please—sit down.' She flushed, glancing awkwardly at Mrs Penworthy and moved towards the table. 'Sorry I'm late.'

She was forced to take the chair beside Michael, because Diane was sitting in the place she usually occupied, and Mrs Penworthy had laid a third place beside her employer. She slid on to the seat, feeling ridiculously that she was intruding, and refused all but coffee when the housekeeper spoke to her.

'Will that be all, then, Mr Tregower?' Mrs Penworthy asked, after filling their cups. 'Are you sure you wouldn't like some ham and eggs? It's not like you——'

'Thank you, Mrs Penworthy.'

Michael's tone brooked no argument, and with a resigned shrug the housekeeper left them. She was ob-

viously curious, and not a little put out by this unexpected turn of events, and Sara wondered what she
was really thinking.

With Mrs Penworthy's departure, Diane withdrew
her attention from the slice of toast on her plate and
fixed Sara with a baleful stare. 'Well?' she said. 'Don't
you think some explanations are in order? Like for
instance, why did you send me that ridiculous telegram?'

'Why did I——?' Sara's eyes widened. 'I never sent
you any telegram.'

'Of course you did——'

'I sent the telegram,' Michael interposed coolly. He
looked at Sara without apology. 'I regret, I was forced
to use your name.'

'My name?'

Sara had scarcely absorbed this before Diane broke
in again, her voice shrill and furious. 'How dare you?'
she snapped, looking at Michael, and then back at the
girl opposite her. 'How dare you bring me down here
on false pretences? How dare you suggest——'

'Adam *is* dead,' declared Michael coldly. 'He died
over a month ago.'

'*What?*'

As Diane slumped back in her chair, shocked for once
out of the complacency of her indifference to anyone's
feelings but her own, Sara turned to Michael again.
'My name?' she echoed. 'What—what did the telegram
say?'

Michael shrugged, his eyes coldly appraising. 'That
Adam was dead, of course. I knew that was the only
thing that might bring some reaction.'

'But you said——'

'I meant what I said,' he declared flatly, and Sara's eyes clung to his, mesmerised by the sudden dilation of his pupils.

'Who are you?'

Diane's choked demand severed the tenuous connection, and with a wry shrug, Michael turned back to her. 'Don't you know?' he taunted, meeting her bewildered stare. 'Don't you have any idea? Did Adam never mention me?'

'The—the stepbrother?' Diane faltered faintly, and Michael inclined his head in mocking assent.

'Adam's half-brother, actually,' he corrected her. 'We had the same father.'

'Yes ...' Diane was obviously striving for control. 'I—I vaguely remember your name being mentioned. But weren't you in South America or somewhere? We never saw you.' She frowned as another thought struck her. 'And—and if Adam is dead——' Her voice broke off abruptly. 'It must have been you—you who sent that message!'

'What message, Diane?' It was Sara who spoke now, indignation giving her a defence she had not known she possessed. 'You said the house was empty, remember? What did Michael say in that message that frightened you so much you had to send me in your place?'

For a moment, Diane was nonplussed. For once in her life she could find no glib answer to the question, and she gazed into Sara's accusing face with tightly clenched lips.

'You thought Adam was here, didn't you?' Sara went on, her own words uneven as she strove for breath. 'You sent me here believing he meant you some—some harm! Dear heaven, Diane, didn't you care what happened to me? Didn't you care what Michael might do?'

Diane cleared her throat, plucking at the rope of pearls that were knotted in the hollow between her breasts. 'You were not in any danger, Sara,' she countered, succeeding in halting the other girl's tremulous flow. 'It seems to me, my dear, that the situation has not worked out entirely to your disadvantage, or we wouldn't be sitting here discussing it now, would we?'

Sara flushed then, but as if taking pity on her, Michael intervened once more. 'You really believed Adam would threaten you, did you, Diane?'

'What else was I to believe—Michael?' Her words were defiant, but watching her, Sara could see the deepening of colour below the cowled neckline of her cashmere sweater, the revealing line that ran up behind her ears, turning them pink at the tips. Knowing her as well as she did, Sara knew Diane was by no means as controlled as she would like to appear, and obviously whatever Michael had said in that message was still relevant so far as she was concerned.

Michael, for his part, was infinitely more relaxed. Sara envied the unhurried way he spooned sugar into his cup, the coolness with which he placed one of his narrow cigars between his teeth. There was the patience of the predator about him, and recalling his fury over his brother's death, she wondered if he could be as indifferent as he seemed.

The silence was ominous, and Sara's nerves stretched. It was all too easy to remember her own fear of him, particularly after the row they had just had, and his scathing denunciation of her own character. What did she know about him, after all? Only what she instinctively felt, what her emotions told her. He could be as clever an actor as Diane, and she no more than a useful pawn in his hands. But would he have proposed to a pawn? she wondered anxiously. Or was even that proposition suspect in the light of his present attitude?

'How—how did you get here, Diane?' she found herself asking suddenly, anything to dispel the feelings of unease that filled her. But it wasn't pity for Diane that motivated her words. Whatever Michael was, whatever he had done, she loved him, and she could not— she *would not*—stand by and allow him to ruin his life without a fight. Diane simply was not worth it. If he was planning revenge, then let it be a more subtle one. Adam was dead, and destroying Diane would not bring him back to life again.

'I flew to Penzance,' Diane answered now, between taut lips. 'I'm flying back this afternoon. Why?' She paused significantly, glancing at Michael. 'Do you want to come with me, Sara?'

'I—I——'

'Sara stays,' declared Michael flatly, before she could gather her thoughts. 'We have some—unfinished business.'

'Do you?' Even as Sara turned to gaze at him, wide-eyed, Diane spat the words, resentment bringing a tremulous anger to her speech. 'The—business—I interrupted upstairs, I suppose.' Her lips curled contemptuously now. 'Oh, my dear, I never thought you could be so stupid!'

'Shut up!' It was Michael who answered her, his features drawn into a grim line. 'Sara doesn't need any advice from you.' He had lit his cigar and now he exhaled smoke into the air above their heads. 'She's a normal, feeling human being—not something you would know a lot about.'

'Oh, really?' Diane's fists clenched on the table beside her plate. 'And you do, I suppose.'

'More than you, Diane, more than you.' His tawny eyes were menacing. 'Sara knows how I feel. She knows how I reacted when I thought she was you——'

'You thought—— oh, *no*!' Diane was incredulous now, deliberately trying to turn his anger aside. 'But how aggravating for you.'

Aggravating! Sara felt a sob of hysteria in the back of her throat and gulped it away. Had Diane really no conception of what Michael had intended?

'It was, rather,' Michael answered now, his tone ominously mild. 'But, as you pointed out earlier, it was not entirely to our—disadvantage.'

Diane licked her lips again. 'Look isn't this all a little—intense? I mean, Adam's dead. I'm sorry. But what more can I say?'

Sara had to admire her courage, but she was alarmed by the darkening of Michael's expression. 'You could have gone to see him,' he retorted harshly. 'He wrote to you. He begged you to come. But you ignored all his letters.'

'I was busy. I was working.' Diane defended herself with appealing candour. 'Michael, I'm an actress. I can't just—abandon my commitments. Surely you can see that. You're a reasonable man, I'm sure. Adam and I were separated. We had nothing left to say to one another.'

'You left him,' said Michael bleakly. 'And his appeals to you were at Christmas. Are you telling me that actresses work all over Christmas? I don't believe it.'

Diane shifted uncomfortably beneath his withering

stare. 'I—I hate illness. I can't stand sickrooms. Adam knew that. He—he would understand——'

'Would he?' Michael spoke scathingly. 'Adam took his own life, that's how much he understood! He killed himself with your tainted image clutched in his bloody hand!'

'No!'

Diane was horrified, but Michael was merciless. 'Yes,' he insisted, his mouth twisting almost pleasurably as he watched her visible disintegration. 'He didn't want to live, knowing you no longer cared about him. He climbed into his bath and slashed his wrists with a shaving mirror. There was blood—blood everywhere!'

'Oh, *no*!' Diane almost moaned the words, her face pale and almost as tormented as his. The ugly word-picture he had painted seemed to have knocked her sick, and she lifted a shaking hand to cup her mouth, as if afraid she might vomit at the table. Even Sara could not deny the twinge of pity she felt for her, a fleeting wave of sympathy for the guilt Diane must be feeling. Michael's verbal castigation would have shaken anyone, let alone someone as emotionally volatile as Diane, and for a few moments she shared her burden. Michael had not said these things to her, she realised belatedly, and she briefly wondered why not. He must have intended to, they were a damning indictment, but for some reason he had remained silent.

Now, he thrust back his chair from the table and got to his feet, and both girls looked up at him with varying degrees of apprehension. He inhaled deeply on the cigar, as if giving himself time to formulate his next words, and then, when Sara's pulse had begun to palpitate alarmingly, he spoke again, his voice heavy but no longer threatening.

'You will have realised by now that I no longer intend to enforce my own kind of justice,' he said.

'You don't?' Diane's voice was faint, but he heard her and shook his head.

'No. Time—and circumstances——' he flicked a glance at Sara, but she averted her eyes, 'have served to moderate my desire for revenge. You're free to go. I won't stop you.'

Diane cleared her throat. It was a nervous sound, made the more so when she attempted to rise to her feet, and in so doing overbalanced her chair. It fell noisily to the floor, and Sara could feel the waves of resentment emanating from her as she bent to pick it up. Diane didn't like to be at a disadvantage, and Sara guessed she would already be seeking some way to turn the situation to suit herself.

'Tell me,' she said then, when the chair was safely restored to its feet, 'was this the only reason why you sent for me? Or is there something else I should know?' She looked interrogatively at Sara. 'I thought perhaps—after what has apparently happened——'

Now it was Sara's turn to get to her feet. 'You've been very fortunate, Diane,' she declared, realising she had to divert the course of the conversation somehow. 'You used me as a scapegoat, as bait in a trap of your own making! Don't try to patronise me now.'

'My dear! I wouldn't dream of it.' Diane's eyes were cold chips of ice. 'I can see you don't need any help from me. You've—er—made your bed, as they say. I just hope you're going to enjoy lying on it.'

Sara was aware of Michael's eyes upon them, but she was no more able to play his game than she was Diane's. The easiest—the *safest*—solution would be to leave Ravens Mill, as soon as possible. But not with Diane.

Their friendship was over. She had driven herself from London; she could drive back again, just as soon as Diane had left.

'I'm an adult, Diane,' she said now, her hands balled at her sides. 'I don't need anyone's permission for—for anything.'

'Of course not.' Diane slanted a malicious glance at Michael. 'I'm sure you both know what you're taking on.'

'I've asked Sara to marry me,' Michael said abruptly, his hand closing possessively on her shoulder. His mouth curled in sudden irony. 'That should relieve your mind, Diane. I'm sure you care what happens to her.'

Sara's knees shook. She had never expected his backing, not after what he had said upstairs, and while she appreciated his support, it was the last thing she wanted him to say in Diane's hearing. Particularly after her humiliation at his hands.

'But—but I've refused,' she burst out recklessly, now uncaring in that moment of agonised alarm how that might sound to him. 'I—I've explained, I don't want to marry anyone. And—and that's all there is to it.'

There was a poignant pause, like a requiem for the brief spell of freedom she had enjoyed, and then Diane spoke, as Sara had known she would.

'Well, that's doubtless for the best, my dear, isn't it?' she drawled. 'After all, no man wants an invalid for a wife, and Michael was probably only offering marriage because he felt obligated to do so!'

CHAPTER NINE

'You couldn't be more wrong!' Michael's crisp tones rang in the awful silence that followed Diane's spiteful revelation. 'Sara's——illness——is nothing to be ashamed of.' His eyes darkened. 'Nor is it something to be brought out and disparaged like some pitiful skeleton in the cupboard. I'm sorry to disappoint you, Diane, but you're telling me nothing new.'

Sara gathered her scattered senses, as Diane's face revealed her utter incredulity. This was the last thing she had expected, Sara guessed correctly, and her own weakening relief was tempered by the awareness that Diane had not gone yet. There was still time for her to say something else, something that would destroy for ever Michael's assumption that she was talking about an attack of asthma.

'You know?' Diane was saying now in arrant disbelief. 'You mean—she told you?' She turned malicious eyes in Sara's direction. 'That's new!'

'I found out,' stated Michael flatly. 'Now, I think you'd better leave before you say something I can't forgive. Adam's solicitors will be contacting you in London, once I give them clearance, and if there's any complication, you can always contact me via the company in Coimbra.'

'I see.' Diane looked at each of them in turn, her eyes narrowed and calculating. 'And I suppose you're set to inherit Adam's share of the business.'

'Adam had no—share in the business, as such,' replied Michael, with immaculate control. 'Goodbye, Diane. I doubt I'll see you again, and if I have anything to do with it, nor will Sara!'

'Ah, but Sara isn't going to marry you, is she, Michael?' Diane drawled, pushing her luck to its limits. 'And despite your—rather touching championship, Sara needs all the friends she can get.'

'With friends like you, she doesn't need enemies,' retorted Michael caustically. 'Oh, get out of here, Diane, before the urge I have to get my hands around your neck becomes irresistible!'

Diane hesitated, but something in Michael's expression now warned her that he was not joking. However, she transferred her attention to Sara as she walked towards the door, saying casually: 'I saw Tony Fielding on Tuesday, Sara. I think he'd been trying to ring you. I told him you'd be back from the country within the next few days.'

Sara's lips parted in dismay. *Tony!* The reason she had been so eager to come down here. It seemed weeks, rather than days, since she had thought about him, and she realised now how trivial their relationship had been. Thinking of him, she felt nothing but indifference, and a faint incredulity that she had imagined she cared for him. He had been there, that was all, and after years of her mother's protection she had responded to his admiration, as a prisoner starved of food might grasp at the first crust of bread.

Aware of Michael's intent gaze, Sara moved her shoulders in an offhand gesture. 'Tony and I have nothing more to say to one another,' she said. 'Thank you for the message, but Tony and I are through.'

'As you like.' Diane subjected them both to a brooding scrutiny. Then she shrugged. 'Well, at least com-

ing here seems to have taught you a lesson, Sara. Adam
and I never had any children, and look what happened
to us!'

'You're beginning to bore me, Diane!'

Michael's voice was curt, but she ignored him, going
on: 'Oh, I know I had my career, and that was—*is*—
important to me. But perhaps, if we'd had a family—
children.' Her eyes narrowed vindictively. 'You have
explained that you can't have children, haven't you,
Sara? Or at least, that it would be highly dangerous
to take that risk? I wonder ...' Her tongue appeared
with provocative consideration. 'Are females in your
condition allowed to take the pill!' Her smile was
pure malice. 'Ah, well, never mind. What a pity it was
such a short acquaintance, Michael. I'm sure we have
more in common than you think.'

She was gone before they could detain her. Not that
Sara wanted to, but somehow, looking at Michael's
stormy features, she guessed he would demand a more
detailed explanation. And from her!

It was too much. Diane's sudden appearance had
been hard enough to bear. Her departure created difficulties Sara did not think she had the stamina to
face. If only she had never gone into Michael's bedroom that morning! If only she had packed her bags
as she had intended to do, she might have got away
before Diane appeared to reduce her to the enfeebled
idiot she felt now.

Without saying a word, she hurried out of the room,
crossing the hall and hastening up the stairs with a
feeling of near panic. She just wanted to get away, to
be on her own for a while, and when he came after
her into the hall and called her name with evident
impatience, she ignored him.

He followed her, of course. She had known he would, even though she had prayed that he would not. After all, he had a right to an explanation, and he was not a man used to taking insolence from anyone. He was angry, and there was not the slightest chance of her getting away without having this out with him.

In her bedroom, she tugged her suitcase from the wardrobe and threw it on to the bed. Then she pulled open the drawers of the dressing table and proceeded to transfer all her belongings into the case. He came to stand in the doorway as she was rolling sweaters into unwieldy bundles, and she spared him a fleeting glance before continuing with her task.

'What are you doing?' he enquired, his voice as controlled as it had been when he spoke to Diane. 'Where do you think you're going?'

'You—you know what and—and where,' she got out unevenly. 'I—I can't stay here. Not now. And—and besides, there's no point, is there? I mean, it was good while it lasted, but——'

She broke off with a gasp as his hand fastened around her throat, almost enclosing it within his long-fingered grasp. 'Stop it!' he snapped savagely, his breathing almost as laboured as hers. 'I don't know what all that was about downstairs, but I sure as hell intend to! What did she mean? Why did she say you can't have children? This is the first time I've heard that an asthmatic shouldn't get pregnant!'

'You're—hurting—me, Michael ...' Her voice was only a squeaky echo of its normally husky tone, but he was unmoved by her plea.

'I can hurt you a whole lot more than this, if you don't tell me the truth!' he muttered, tightening his fingers purposefully. 'For God's sake, Sara. Don't I have a right to know?'

Sara moved her head helplessly from side to side, trying to escape his bruising hold, and with a stifled oath, he relaxed his grasp. His fingers seemed to respond to the softness of her skin, and obviously against his will, he was consumed by the haunting beauty of her eyes.

'Sara ...' he groaned hoarsely, and it required all her powers of resistance to move out of his reach. But she did it, putting protective hands to her throat, feeling the tenderness of her throbbing flesh.

'What do you want me to tell you?' she asked at last, her voice still choked and raw. 'Why should it matter to you what Diane was implying? I've said I won't marry you, so you have no cause for concern, one way or the other. In any case, she was lying. No one has ever told me I should not have a child.'

That at least was true, but Michael did not look as if he believed her. On the contrary, he looked strained and drawn, confusion pulling down the corners of his mouth and bringing a deep crease to his forehead. Her heart went out to him in his pain and bewilderment, but whatever his feelings, she could not take what could never be hers.

'What is wrong with you, Sara?' he demanded now, staring at her with tortured eyes. 'Is it only asthma? Or is there something else? For God's sake, you can trust me. I only want to make you happy.'

'What else could there be?' she countered, pushing shoes into plastic bags and stowing them in corners. 'Michael, please! We've said all there is to say. It was said before Diane chose to make her comments. Why can't you accept that I don't want to get married— for whatever reason?'

Michael expelled his breath noisily. 'You're determined to leave, then?'

'Yes.'

'Only this morning, you said——'

'That was before.'

'Before Diane came.'

'No.' She sighed. 'Before you started talking about
getting married. Oh, Michael, you'll soon forget about
me. You said yourself, there have been other women...'

'There has.' His words were cutting and violent. 'But
I never cared about any of them—until now!' He gave
a short, mirthless laugh. 'Well, this should teach me
not to be so reckless in future.'

Sara winced, but he didn't touch her again. Instead
he turned and left the room, and presently she heard
the outer door slam also. He had gone. Where, she
didn't know, but the knowledge that she might never
see him again almost achieved what his fingers had
not. What price pride, now? she wondered bitterly.
Would it have been fairer to tell him the truth? She
would never know. One thing was certain, she would
never suffer the pangs of remorse that would come
once their marriage started to go sour. As it surely
would, once pity gave way to frustration, and sympathy
to resentment.

She finished packing without haste. She guessed he
would not come back until she had left the house, and
she carried her own suitcases down the stairs with an
aching heart. To think she had come here to escape
from one impossible situation, and wound up with an
infinitely more impossible one.

It was raining in London, not a clean, drenching down-
pour but a steady, uninspiring drizzle, that fell from

a low-hanging, leaden sky. The flat that Sara had moved into after her mother's death was dull and uninspiring, too, and the first few days she was back home she missed the open spaces she was used to seeing from the windows. She missed the cries of the sea-birds, and the continuous thunder of the ocean, muted below the craggy cliffs; but most of all she missed the excitement of Michael's presence in the house, and the unpredictability of their relationship.

Tony had phoned, as Diane predicted, and Sara wondered whether her absence had affected his feelings. Perhaps he had realised her potential in terms of a listener, Tony could be an awful bore at times, particularly when it came to photography, or maybe he really had missed her. Whatever, she had halted his flow of facile pleasantries with polite but cutting firmness, and replaced her receiver feeling a little mean, but definitely relieved.

Her return to the office was heralded with a seasonable overflow of work. Her own manuscript had been stored away again, in lieu of the day she could really settle down to it, and she tried to submerge herself in other people's contributions. Reading was, at least, an escape, and for hours at a time she could hold her painful thoughts at bay. Nevertheless, the strain took its toll on her, and Arthur Stringer, her boss, was not slow to notice the fact.

'Where was this place you went for that holiday?' he asked, coming into her office one morning to find her slumped on two elbows, pouring over a manuscript loosely based on a presidential assassination. 'Cornwall?' He shook his head. 'Well, it doesn't seem to have done you much good. You look positively drained!'

'I'm all right, honestly.' Sara sat up, pushing back

the weight of her hair with a hasty hand, and forcing a smile to her lips. 'But all this rain ...' She indicated the wet day beyond the double-glazed windows. 'It's so depressing.'

'Hmm.' Stringer frowned, positioning himself in front of her, arms folded like some mediaeval inquisitor. 'You're sure that's all it is? You've not been overdoing things? I mean,' he paused significantly, 'I heard about you and Fielding. I believe you used to be quite close.'

'Oh, I see.'

Sara lay back in her chair, stretching her arms above her head, unconsciously drawing his attention to the rounded curve of her breasts, the burgeoning fullness, that swelled against the thin silk of her navy shirt. Stringer had always been aware of her in the office, of her quiet intelligence and unassuming personality, but never before had he been so sensible to her latent sexuality, to an innate femininity about her that seemed curiously to have been awakened. He was a married man, after all, with a wife and three sturdy sons to his credit, but for once he felt a stirring of emotion that had nothing to do with the paternal attitude he usually adopted towards her. Was Fielding responsible for this? He couldn't believe it. But she had definitely changed since her holiday in the West Country, and even the lines of weariness around her eyes had a languorous attraction all their own.

'You can tell me to mind my own business, if you like,' he was continuing, when she lowered her arms again and said:

'My association with Tony Fielding ended weeks ago, Arthur. Oh, I admit, I was pretty upset at the time, but since then ...' She paused. 'As it happens, he rang me a couple of days ago. I told him I didn't want to see him any more.'

Stringer sighed. 'He found out, didn't he? About— well, about your heart condition.'

Sara nodded, without rancour. 'Diane told him. I suppose she did me a favour.'

'Huh!' Stringer snorted. 'I doubt that was her intention. But never mind. So—you really are okay?'

'Okay,' Sara echoed, resting her elbows on her desk again. 'But it was nice of you to ask. I appreciate that.'

Stringer hesitated. He was a squat man, square and sturdy, with a mat of curly brown hair and a long, intelligent face. In his forties now, he had started with the firm when he was a teenager, and had risen to the position of Managing Director. Yet for all that he had never lost his Derbyshire accent, or his consideration for every member of their staff. He was well liked, and popular among his contemporaries, and there had never been a shred of scandal attached to his name, even though he met some of the most successful women writers in the world. But at this moment he had an almost overwhelming impulse to lay it all on the line, and ask this young woman to have lunch with him.

'Sara . . .' He leant forward, resting his square capable hands on the edge of her desk, regarding her with restless intensity. 'Sara, if there's anything I can do . . .'

'There's not.' Her cool response sobered him, and with a feeling of impotence he left it there.

After he had gone, however, Sara could not deny the faintly warming sensation, deep inside her. Arthur cared, she thought in amazement. He really cared what happened to her. The world was not such a harsh place, after all.

Two days later Diane telephoned.

Sara had half expected her to do so, and her immediate impulse was to replace the receiver without responding, but Diane was ready for that.

'I've seen Michael,' she said at once, and although she knew she was all kinds of a fool, Sara had to answer her.

'You—have?' she queried, striving for nonchalance, while her mind fragmented with images of Michael and Diane together. 'So? Why are you telling me?'

'Oh, come on ...' Diane was not to be put off that easily. 'Don't pretend it doesn't interest you, because I just don't believe it. You're interested all right. Would you like to know why he came to see me?'

'Not particularly.' Sara's voice was tight now, but she couldn't help it. 'Was it something to do with Adam's will? I believe he owned Ravens Mi——'

'It wasn't to do with Adam!' declared Diane tersely. 'Do you honestly think Michael cares whether or not I own Ravens Mill or he does?' She hesitated. 'No. It was to do with you.'

'Me?' Sara almost squeaked the word, and Diane said: 'Yes, you!' with sardonic irony.

Sara's palm was moist against the handpiece of the receiver. Michael had gone to see Diane? About her? She could guess why, but what had Diane told him?

'Don't you want to know what he wanted?' Diane asked now, echoing her thoughts, and realising it was better to be forewarned, Sara forced a low murmur of assent. 'He wanted to ask me about you—about your condition,' Diane continued. 'Apparently you'd given him some story about having asthma. Asthma! I ask you. Honestly, Sara, couldn't you do better than that?'

Sara's legs gave out on her, and she sought the comfort of her couch. 'But you—told him the truth, of

course?' she whispered weakly, and Diane's scornful
laughter was answer enough.

'My dear, what else could I do? Faced with the man!
I mean, I didn't know what pitiful little story you'd
trumped up. Heavens, I assumed he knew! I thought
all he'd come to me for was the details. You know—
how serious it is, and what the chances of living a
normal life are.'

'And—and what did he say?' Sara had to know. She
had to hear how he had reacted. At least from Diane
she could be sure of learning the worst.

'Well ...' Diane considered her words, 'he was
shocked naturally. And maybe a little—relieved.'

'Relieved?'

'Of course. Darling, can you imagine his feelings?
He'd asked you to marry him. I suppose he was realising what a lucky escape he'd had.'

Sara gasped at this, and as if regretting the callousness of her words, Diane tried to make amends. 'Well,
dear, it has to be faced, hasn't it? No man—particularly a man as—well, strong and virile as Michael
Tregower, wants to be tied to an invalid for the rest of
his life.' She made a sound of impatience, before continuing: 'I must say he's not at all like his brother.
What a pity he was in South America when I met
Adam. He and I are much more alike than Adam and
I ever were. We know what we want, and we go and get
it. I couldn't honestly see him allowing me the freedom
Adam did, and who knows, I might have been a better
person because of it.' She paused. 'Still, there's world
enough and time, as they say.'

Sara's throat felt choked. 'You mean—you mean——'

'Oh, darling, don't be silly.' Diane laughed again.
'Right now, all my handsome brother-in-law wants to

do is to get out of England, as quickly as possible. He hasn't even *seen* me—yet. But we are related, and whether he likes it or not, Adam did have shares in the Los Santos Mining Corporation. So you see ...'

Her voice trailed away, and Sara sat there, holding the telephone, mesmerised by what she had just heard. She had thought she couldn't be hurt any more, but she was wrong, terribly wrong. She felt shattered, absolutely shattered, and more depressed than she had ever felt in her life before.

'Sara! *Sara!*' There was a note of anxiety in Diane's voice now, and realising she had to say something, Sara took a deep painful breath.

'Yes?'

'Oh, you're still there, thank goodness.' Diane sounded relieved. 'I only wanted to add one more thing ...'

'What is it?'

'Well—just that I'd like to see you again Sara——'

'No!'

'Listen to me!' Diane was appealing now. 'Sara, you can't blame me for what's happened. It wasn't my fault.'

'You sent me to Ravens Mill,' insisted Sara dully, but Diane continued to protest.

'I didn't know Michael was there, did I? I thought Adam——'

'Adam!' Sara's voice was bitter. 'Poor Adam! I know how you must have felt.'

'Sara!' Diane sounded horrified. 'My God, you wouldn't—*no*. No, you wouldn't. Sara, no man is worth it, believe me, I know. Even Adam had his revenge of sorts. And there was I terrified because I thought he might—might——'

'Might *what*, Diane?' Sara forced the words from her lips. 'Exactly what did you think Adam might do?'

Diane heaved a sigh. 'Well, I suppose it doesn't matter now. He—that is, Michael—wrote me a letter, describing among other things the chemical reaction of—of sulphuric acid on—on human flesh!'

'Oh, no!' Sara was horrified now. 'And you let me——'

'I had my career to think of,' Diane pleaded urgently. 'Try to put yourself in my place, Sara. If—if I'd been disfigured—besides,' she added quickly, 'a blind man could hardly be completely accurate.'

'You've just thought of that,' exclaimed Sara accusingly.

'Adam would know you were not me,' insisted Diane.

'How? He was blind, as you said. How could he have known? Unless he was prepared to give me a chance to speak for myself.'

'It's all supposition anyway. Adam was dead——'

'You didn't know that.'

'Oh, Sara——'

But Sara had replaced her receiver, shocked and sick to her stomach. Diane was completely unscrupulous, selfish and self-centred. Why hadn't she realised it until now? Why hadn't she been able to see what everyone else appeared to have known all along?

With nausea rising in her throat, she stumbled into the bathroom and relieved herself at the basin. She seldom was sick, but right now, all she could think of was what might have happened if Michael had been as cruel and unscrupulous as Diane.

There were times during the following days when she was desperately tempted to confide in Arthur Stringer.

In a world of hostile faces, he seemed the only friend she had. But in spite of his kindness she had seen something else in his expression, and she had more emotional complications than she could deal with as it was. She didn't blame Michael. It was what she had expected, after all. But somehow she had expected pity, not revulsion.

It was stupid, she knew, particularly after the way she had acted, but there had been times when she had believed she might see him again. It had just been a tiny glimmer of hope, but now even that had been extinguished, and she felt terribly alone.

Time, however, had its own methods of healing, and by the end of the second week she had almost convinced herself that if Michael had been so easily deterred, he could not—*he could never have been*—the man she had imagined him to be. Cold comfort, but how could she have loved someone who never even existed? she asked herself logically, and then cried herself to sleep because love was illogical.

The weather eventually changed, and with the disappearance of the rain, the sun came to brighten London's grey streets. Sara determinedly took to walking home from work, telling herself that the exercise would do her good, and ignoring the persistent small voice inside her that chided her efforts to exhaust her too-vivid imagination. But how could she not think of Michael and what he might be doing, particularly when Diane's play folded at the Tabasco, and it was stated in the papers that she was going to take a long holiday?

There were flower-sellers at every street corner, and sometimes Sara bought herself a bunch of anemones or violets, burying her nose in their fragrance, trying to recapture her love of simple things she had once taken for granted. How long ago those days seemed, when she had known peace of mind. Was it really Tony who had changed all that, or had it been an inevitable progression? If being hurt was part of living, why should she have imagined she would be immune?

One evening, about a month after her return from Cornwall, she rounded the corner of Dolphin Grove to find a dark brown Mini parked on the double yellow lines outside the flats. It was unusual to find any cars parked in Dolphin Grove. An adequate underground parking area had been provided for the use of the tenants of Dolphin Court, and visitors invariably parked in the adjoining thoroughfare, where there were parking meters. Still, it was nothing to do with her if someone chose to run the risk of confronting an irate traffic warden, and she entered the building with a characteristic shrug of her slim shoulders.

Her eyes were blinded for a moment by the sudden change from sunlight to shadowy interior, but she saw the silhouette of the man who stepped into her path, and her heart leapt suffocatingly into her throat. Blinking in disbelief, she gazed up at him, then shook her head rapidly as he reached for her.

'Sara . . .' His voice was just as disruptively sensual as she remembered, his open-necked denim shirt and tight-fitting jeans accentuating his powerful masculinity. 'Oh, Sara, it's been too long . . .'

Sara's hands sought his upper arms, holding him off with what little resistance she had. She had to fight the urge to surrender to his eager embrace, but she realised how puny her efforts would be if he chose to impose his will. Nevertheless she had to make the attempt, though her voice shook as she said tightly: 'What are you doing here, Michael? How did you get my address? I thought we agreed——'

'We didn't agree anything,' he corrected her dryly, his hands at her waist warm through the thin cotton shirt she was wearing. 'Now, can we go somewhere more private? I have things to say to you.'

'No!' Sara tried to draw back from him. 'I mean, there's nothing to say. It's all been said. Please—I'm hot and tired. I need a shower and a change of clothes. I think it would be much better if you left—right now.'

Michael shook his head. 'Sorry, but I have no intention of leaving here until you and I have had time to sort things out. Now, do we go to your flat, or do I have to take you to my hotel room? It's all the same to me.'

Sara glanced behind her. 'That's—*your* Mini out there?'

'That's right.'

'But it's a no-parking area.'

'Big deal.' Michael's tone was ironic. 'Sara—*love*!' She quivered at the husky endearment. 'Don't let's waste any more time. I know about your heart condition, and that's what I want to talk to you about. But not here. Not in this public lobby, a source of entertainment to anyone who passes through!'

Sara licked her lips. His words were a powerful inducement, and she longed to give in to him. It would be so much easier to let him have his way with her, so much more desirable, but wasn't she only compounding her foolishness? So he knew about her illness. What did that mean? What difference did it make? Only that Diane had been wrong when she said he had been eager to leave the country. Or perhaps he had left, and come back again. Perhaps he had had second thoughts ... Whatever his reason for being here, they did not alter the impossibility of the situation.

'Michael,' she began again, 'I—I'm flattered that— that you still want to see me, but——'

'*God!*' His temper erupted violently. 'Sara, give me your key. The key to your flat, yes. Where is it? In your handbag?' He jerked the leather purse out of her hands and opened it forcefully, the contents rattling together noisily as he rummaged for her key ring. 'Are these them? Yes? Good. Shall we take the lift?'

Sara felt powerless to resist his overwhelming determination. It was all very well berating herself for giving in to his demands, but short of running away from him, what else could she do? He was bigger than she was, and infinitely stronger, and sooner or later he was bound to get his own way. She could only hope her spirit was less fickle than her flesh.

CHAPTER TEN

HER flat was on the second floor, high above the central grove of poplars that gave the close its name. It was not big—just a bedroom and a living room, with a tiny kitchenette attached, and the use of a bathroom shared with the flat next door. An elderly spinster lived next door, who taught at the local primary school. She was a pleasant enough individual, but like Sara, she kept very much to herself, and they seldom met.

Michael fitted Sara's key into the lock, and the door swung open into her small living room. Fortunately, the flats were let unfurnished, and Sara had been able to keep the best pieces of furniture from her mother's house after it had been sold. The chairs that flanked the gas fireplace were upholstered in squashy green leather, and there were one or two good pictures on the plain emulsioned walls. Even the carpet underfoot was springy, and the choice of furnishings reflected Sara's good taste. Despite its size, it was an attractive room, and she was glad she did not have to feel ashamed of it.

Michael allowed her to precede him into the flat, and then followed her more slowly, closing the door behind him. He was obviously intrigued by his surroundings, and she saw his eyes flickering over the old-fashioned gateleg table that stood against the wall, and the writing bureau, with its rosewood marquetry, which was so distinctive. His presence dwarfed the room, however, and she thought how cramped it must seem to him after the generously proportioned rooms he was probably used to.

'So this is where you've been living since your mother died,' he observed reflectively, straightening away from the door, and as she puzzled how he knew so much about her, he caught her by the shoulders and jerked her into his arms. 'So long,' he muttered, against her startled mouth. 'Too long ... much too long ...' and she felt her resistance fade beneath the searching hunger of his lips.

He kissed her many times, short passionate kisses, moving his mouth from one side of hers to the other, until she turned her face up to his, like a flower seeking the warmth of the sun, their lips meeting and clinging as if they would never let go. Her senses were swimming, her breathing was shallow and laboured, but then so was his, and his hands that tugged her shirt from the waistband of her skirt and spread against the column of her spine were hotly possessive.

'Sara,' he groaned, when she could feel the hardening length of him against her. 'I'll never let you go again. Never!' And she had no will to deny the revealing response of her own body.

But with her weak and yielding against him, Michael lifted his head, pushing back the damp hair from her forehead, allowing his thumbs to move caressingly over her temples and the heated contours of her cheeks. He seemed to get an immense amount of satisfaction out of just looking at her, and although she was not unused to his appraisal, she could not help the feelings of self-consciousness it aroused. What was he thinking? she wondered anxiously. Was he searching for some revealing trait of her condition, or was he regretting already his impulse to come here after her?

'How are you?' he asked at last, lowering his lips to her forehead and allowing his tongue to caress the moist flesh. 'Have you missed me? Lie, if you have to, but don't tell me you haven't.'

'Oh, Michael ...' With a sob she collapsed against him, burying her face against the hair-roughened skin of his chest, exposed now that she had unbuttoned his shirt. 'Michael, why did you come here? Don't you know this is the cruellest thing you could do to me? I—I tried to keep it simple, but you—you've complicated everything. Why did you do it? Why did you do it?'

'Hey!' His fingers found her chin and forced it upwards, making her look at him through the tear-drenched veil of her lashes. 'I came here because I love you, because I suspected you—loved me.' His eyes bored into hers, dark and passionate. 'You do, don't you? Oh, Sara, you fool! You crazy fool! Did you really think your condition would change the way I felt?'

Sara sniffed. 'It does. It has to. Michael, I don't have the right to marry anyone.'

'That's ridiculous!' His hands cupped her face with painful intensity. 'Sara, I am going to marry you, believe me. And I don't care what nonsense Diane has filled your head with.'

'Diane?' Sara was dazed, looking up at him. 'What else did she tell you?'

'What else?' His brows descended. 'Diane told me nothing, Sara. Nothing! She let me go on thinking you had asthma, guessing, I suppose, that I was less likely to come looking for you if I was convinced there was nothing seriously wrong with you. What a blessing my ego wouldn't let me believe her!'

'But——' Sara couldn't believe it. 'She—she said——'

'Yes?' He was impatient. 'What did she say? I should have guessed she'd contact you.'

'She—she did.' Sara licked her dry lips. 'She—told me that you—that you'd been—well, shocked, when you learned that I—that I——'

'*God!* The bitch!' Michael swore angrily. 'What else did she tell you? Did she explain that she wouldn't give me your address? That I had to find out where you worked from the man who broke up my half-brother's marriage?'

'Lance?' Sara was shocked. 'But—but——'

'I went to see him,' stated Michael flatly. 'I hoped he might know you, and then I found out he was your father's cousin or something, and he knew as much about you as Diane did.' He sighed ruefully. 'He was quite decent, actually. I was prepared to detest the man, but I couldn't. I guess he must be a little like you. At any rate, I found him quite charming, and more than a little concerned about you after I explained what Diane had done.'

'You—explained?' Sara was wide-eyed, and Michael nodded without contrition.

'Why not? She was prepared to sacrifice you without compunction. I told him a few home truths, and he seemed very receptive to what I had to say.'

'Oh, Michael!'

'Don't "oh, Michael" me in that rueful way. That woman has ruined one life already, and would have been quite willing to ruin two more. Why should I feel sorry for her? Anyway,' his lips twitched a little, 'you might not feel so sympathetic towards her if I tell you she wouldn't have been averse to my taking up where Adam left off.'

Sara gasped. 'What do you mean?'

'What do you think I mean?'

'You didn't——.'

'No, I didn't,' he agreed reassuringly, bending his head to part her lips with his. 'Mmm, jealousy tastes so sweet!'

Sara trembled, but her arms were around his waist, and she did not draw back when his kiss hardened into passion. She was giving up so much, she thought despairingly. Surely she had the right to take this small consolation.

'So ...' he muttered at last, his voice thickened with emotion. 'Where was I? Oh, yes ...' He blinked, trying to concentrate on what he was saying. 'As I say, I spoke to Wilmer, and he was very enlightening. Apparently he knew all about your condition right from the beginning, and he explained about your getting rheumatic fever when you were a baby, and how the valve was narrowed and how it won't close properly.' He pressed her closer, as if the nearness of his body could act as a protection against the dangers of congestive heart disease. 'He was very sympathetic, and if it's any consolation to you, he gave us his blessing.'

'Michael ...' Sara tried to pull away from him then, but he wouldn't let her go. 'Michael, this doesn't make any difference——,'

'Like hell it doesn't!' he snapped, and then more wearily: 'Okay, okay. Let me finish. There's more, if you insist on hearing it.'

'More?'

'Yes, more.' Michael's face was drawn now. 'Wilmer told me something else. Something you may or may not know about.'

'What?'

Michael sighed. 'Apparently—apparently, after

you'd recovered from that attack of rheumatic fever, your mother became absurdly protective. She kept you with her whenever she could, and never allowed you to do anything that might endanger your health.'

Sara nodded. 'That's right, she did. But she was only thinking of me.'

'Was she?' Michael's mouth pulled down at the corners. 'Did you know, when you were ten years old, she was approached by the specialist who had treated you when you were a baby? Apparently the advances in heart surgery were such that he—the specialist—considered that it might be possible to operate and correct the narrowing of the valve, even install an artificial valve if necessary.'

'*No!*' Sara gulped. 'I don't believe it. She would have told me.'

'Not necessarily. You were only ten years old, remember? The person she did discuss it with was your doctor.'

'Doctor Harding?'

'Harding. Yes, that's right.' Michael paused. 'He recommended against it, and your mother was only too willing to agree.'

'Doctor Harding recommended against it?'

Michael nodded. 'Yes. From what I can gather, he doesn't care much for modern technology.'

'How do you know?'

'Wilmer told me. He went to see him yesterday. He'd also spoken to the surgeon at St Oliver's.'

'St Oliver's?' Sara frowned. 'But that's the hospital where—where——'

'—where you were treated when you had rheumatic fever? I know. The specialist who treated you has retired now, but the man Wilmer spoke to is the present consultant.'

Sara was bewildered. 'But why did Lance go to St Oliver's? Why did he speak to Doctor Harding? I don't understand.'

'Don't you?' Michael sighed. 'No, well, I didn't want him to do it. But he seemed to think it was worth the effort.'

'What effort?' Sara's voice was faint. 'You mean there might be some chance that I could have this operation now?'

Michael hesitated, obviously reluctant to go on. 'Operations are risky things,' he muttered harshly. 'Why can't you accept that I love you just the way you are?'

'Michael!' Sara's features were taut now. 'Please. You have to tell me the truth. If Lance has found something out ...'

'Lance isn't involved, Sara. *We* are.'

'*Michael!*'

'Oh, all right, all right. Livingstone—the surgeon, that is—he believes he might be able to help you.'

Sara gasped. 'Oh, Michael!'

'That's what you wanted to hear, isn't it?' He thrust her away from him then, and paced heavily across the room. 'It doesn't matter to you how I feel, only that you should satisfy whatever devil there is inside you that demands the complete sacrifice! This is open-heart surgery, we're talking about, Sara! Not pulling a tooth. And Doctor Harding is still of the opinion that so long as you don't do anything foolish, you could lead a perfectly reasonable life——'

'A *reasonable* life, yes,' Sara interrupted him. 'Michael, can't you see what this means to me? It may

be an opportunity to lead a *normal* life, not a reasonable one. I love you, you know that: I can't deny it.
But marrying you—it wouldn't be fair. To either of
us.'

'And what about me?' he asked flatly. 'Where do I
stand? Condemned to two impossible choices. Either I
accept that you must take this chance, and in so doing
accept the risk too—or I lose you, because of some hare-
brained belief you have that you'll be a burden to me.'
He pushed back his hair with hands that she saw were
shaking a little. 'I don't know that I can take it. Oh,
when Wilmer first started talking about an operation,
I admit I was impressed. But I soon changed my mind
when we began to discuss the difficulties involved. I
didn't even want him to make enquiries, but—well, I
had to have some reason for contacting you again, so I
let him go ahead. There were things I had to do anyway. Isabella was wanting to know where I was and
what I was doing, and I had to go out there and explain
the situation to her, and by the time I got back, Wilmer
had contacted Livingstone, and you know the rest.' He
made a weary gesture. 'He'd have come here himself to
see you, if I hadn't agreed to tell you.'

Sara trembled. 'But you don't think he was right?'

'I think—*I feel*—that what we have is more important than what may result from some miracle cure,' he
replied quietly. 'All right, so you can't swim the Chan-
nel or run up a mountain! So what? People have been
known to survive without doing either of those things.
And quite happily, too. From what I hear, you've got
a hell of a better chance than most, and the idea of
putting your life in jeopardy for purely—selfish
reasons——'

'Selfish?'

'Who else are you considering?' he demanded harshly, and suddenly there was no doubt in her mind about what she really wanted.

'And—you'd marry me knowing—knowing——'

'I love you!' he ground out angrily. 'Goddammit, I wish I didn't!'

'Oh, Michael ...'

With a little sob she covered the space between them, throwing her arms around him and pressing her body close to his. 'Darling, darling Michael! We're going to be so happy together.'

'What do you mean?'

Incredulity still showed in his expression as she lifted her face to his and touched his cheek with adoring fingers. 'I'll marry you, Michael. Whenever you say. Tomorrow, if you like. I—I only wanted to make you happy, you see. I've lived with this for so long now, but you—you're so strong and healthy, and I thought— oh, I thought if I was well again——'

But her mouth was silenced by the pressure of his, and for a long time there was no sound at all.

They were to be married two weeks later. It was to be a quiet wedding, with few guests, but Michael's great-aunt had promised to make the journey from Coimbra, and Sara's happiness was complete.

Then, a few days before the wedding, she had a telephone call from Lance Wilmer. He had been out of the country, Michael had told her, probably with Diane, she realised now, but he had returned to represent her side of the family at the small church in Kensington where she was to be married. He seemed delighted that she was to find happiness at last, but disappointed that she had not gone to see Livingstone.

'Is that wise, Sara?' he demanded, rekindling the doubts she thought she had succeeded in burying. 'Why don't you at least hear what he has to say? I can make the arrangements—tomorrow, if necessary. Sara, you owe it to yourself.'

Sara shifted her weight from one foot to the other rather uneasily. She was glad Michael was not there to see her indecision. Was she always to know this uncertainty where her health was concerned? How could she agree to something she had promised to forget?

'I'm sorry, Lance,' she said at last. 'It was kind of you to go to all that trouble, but it's not what Michael wants, and I love him too much to risk hurting him again.'

Lance protested again, as she had known he would, but she was adamant, and at last he had to give up. She heard Michael letting himself into the flat with the key she had given him, as she replaced her receiver, and was glad he had not had to hear her refusal. She loved him too much to want to spoil these days before their wedding.

The following afternoon Michael had a surprise for her, however.

'There's someone that I want you to meet,' was all he would say, helping her into the Mini, and she pulled a curious face when he wouldn't be drawn.

But her curiosity was dispelled by other emotions, when he drove through the gates of St Oliver's Hospital, and she turned worried eyes in his direction when he parked the car near the specialised heart unit.

'Michael . . .'

Her mouth was dry and anxious, as she turned to him, but she saw none of the censure in his face she had expected to see.

'I heard what you said to Wilmer yesterday,' he explained gently. 'You thought I came back as you were finishing the call, but I didn't. I heard it all.'

'Then you'll know——'

'I know that I'll have no peace of mind until you're examined by an expert. Until I can satisfy myself that what we're doing is right.'

'But Michael——'

'See him. Do this, for me. Then we'll talk about it, shall we?'

Sara had no choice but to obey, but she walked into the hospital on shaky legs. There was so much she would have liked to say, but there was no time now.

The examination Mr Livingstone subjected her to was extremely thorough. Aware of Michael, sitting in the waiting room, fretting over what might be going to happen, Sara wondered how she could ever have doubted his feelings for her. She knew what a traumatic experience this must be for him. At least she was there, she knew what was going on, whereas Michael had to suffer alone.

It took a long time, or at least that was how it seemed to Sara, but at last Mr Livingstone seemed satisfied with his investigations. After she was dressed again and facing him across the width of his leather-topped desk, he sat for several minutes just looking at her. Then he said quietly:

'Naturally I would have preferred an overnight examination, to give me time to do further tests. But from what I've learned in this short time, I would say you were in reasonably good shape.'

'I am?'

Sara caught her breath as he nodded.

'Yes. Amazingly so, considering.'

'Oh.' Sara didn't know what else to say, and he smiled.

'You do know you're pregnant, don't you?'

Sara gasped. 'No.'

'I'm afraid so.' His tone was dry. 'About six weeks, I would say. Would you agree with that?'

Sara did not know how to answer him. Her discussion with Michael about a hypothetical pregnancy had never really troubled her, but now she realised it could be so.

'But—I thought——'

'You didn't expect it?' Mr Livingstone shrugged. 'Why not? Your reproductive organs are just as efficient as anyone else's.' He paused. 'You're getting married in a few days, aren't you?'

'Well, yes, but——'

'Don't you want a baby?'

Sara clasped her hands. 'Oh, yes!'

'Ah.' Mr Livingstone seemed to understand. 'You're concerned because of your health. Well, I don't think you need to be, so long as you are well cared for. I believe you'll be living in Portugal. As it happens, I know a doctor who works at the university hospital in Lisbon. I can arrange for him to take care of you while you're pregnant. If you wish.'

Sara licked her lips. 'And—and the operation . . .'

'Out of the question, at this time.' He shifted the papers on his desk. 'But don't worry. Come back and see me after your baby's born. That is, if you still want to.' He smiled again. 'Don't look so pleased about it. If all my patients were like you, I'd soon be out of a job!'

Sara could tell from Michael's face that waiting had put a terrific strain on him, and once they were in the car again she was eager to put his mind at rest.

'There's to be no operation,' she told him gently, touching his cheek with loving fingers. 'But thank you for this. You don't know what it means to me.'

Michael captured her hand with his, pulling it to his lips and pressing his face into her palm. Then he lifted tormented eyes to hers. 'Why?' he demanded huskily. 'What did he say?'

'He said I was in pretty good shape,' declared Sara lightly, nestling closer. 'Particularly so, for a pregnant lady.'

'What!' Michael gazed at her disbelievingly. 'Oh—Lord, *no!*'

'Yes.' Sara could understand his anxiety, but she was quick to allay it. 'What's more, he says there's absolutely no reason why I shouldn't have a baby. And he's going to put me in touch with a colleague of his at the hospital in Lisbon, and he'll take over all the necessary treatment.'

Michael shook his head. 'But I thought—oh, Sara, do you really want to go through with this?'

Sara nodded. Then she said hesitantly: 'Why? You do want the baby, don't you?'

Michael's laughter was choked. 'Oh, darling, you know I want whatever you want. And I can think of nothing more delightful than having a daughter like you. But——'

'No buts.' Sara was rather smug. 'To think, I have Diane to thank for this really. I wonder what her reactions will be when she finds out?'

'I wouldn't put it past her to have persuaded Wilmer to come back here and talk to you,' retorted Michael dourly. 'But, as it happens, she did us both a favour.'

'Mmm.' Sara's eyes were tender as they rested on him.

'At least now I know I'm not just a helpless invalid, incapable of being a *real* wife to you.'

'Oh, Sara!' Michael tapped her nose with a teasing finger. 'I never had any doubts on that score!' and her cheeks turned a becoming shade of pink as he started the motor of the car.

Titles available this month in the Mills & Boon ROMANCE Series

RETURN TO DEVIL'S VIEW *by Rosemary Carter*
Jana could only succeed in her search for some vital information by working as secretary to the enigmatic Clint Dubois — and it was clear that Clint suspected her motives . . .

THE MAN ON THE PEAK *by Katrina Britt*
The last thing Suzanne had wanted or expected when she went to Hong Kong for a holiday was to run into her ex-husband Raoul . . .

TOGETHER AGAIN *by Flora Kidd*
Ellen and Dermid Craig had separated, but now circumstances had brought Ellen back to confront Dermid again. Was this her chance to rebuild her marriage, or was it too late?

A ROSE FROM LUCIFER *by Anne Hampson*
Colette had always loved the imposing Greek Luke Marlis, but only now was he showing that he was interested in her. Interested — but not, it seemed, enough to want to marry her . . .

THE JUDAS TRAP *by Anne Mather*
When Sara Fortùne fell in love with Michael Tregower, and he with her, all could have ended happily. Had it not been for the secret that Sara dared not tell him . . .

THE TEMPESTUOUS FLAME *by Carole Mortimer*
Caroline had no intention of marrying Greg Fortnum, whom she didn't even know apart from his dubious reputation — so she escaped to Cumbria where she met the mysterious André . . .

WITH THIS RING *by Mary Wibberley*
Siana had no memory of who she really was. But what were Matthew Craven's motives when he appeared and announced that he was going to help her find herself again?

SOLITAIRE *by Sara Craven*
The sooner Marty got away from Luc Dumarais the better, for Luc was right out of her league, and to let him become important to her would mean nothing but disaster . . .

SWEET COMPULSION *by Victoria Woolf*
Marcy Campion was convinced that she was right not to let Randal Saxton develop her plot of land — if only she could be equally convinced about her true feelings for Randal!

SHADOW OF THE PAST *by Robyn Donald*
Morag would have enjoyed going back to Wharuaroa, where she had been happy as a teenager, if it hadn't meant coming into constant contact with Thorpe Cunningham.

Mills & Boon Romances
– all that's pleasurable in Romantic Reading!

Available September 1979

Forthcoming Mills & Boon Romances

CHATEAU IN THE PALMS by *Anne Hampson*
Philippe de Chameral could have made Jane happy — but he did not know that she was a married woman . . .

SAVAGE POSSESSION by *Margaret Pargeter*
Melissa had been too used to having her own way to allow Ryan Trevelyan to dominate her — but she soon had to change her tune!

ONE MORE RIVER TO CROSS by *Essie Summers*
Rebecca was as different from her flighty cousin Becky as chalk from cheese, but the girls' identical appearance was to get Rebecca into a difficult situation with the bossy Darroch . . .

LURE OF EAGLES by *Anne Mather*
An unknown cousin had inherited the family business, and Domine found herself agreeing to the masterful Luis Aguilar's suggestion that she accompany him to South America to meet the girl.

MIDNIGHT SUN'S MAGIC by *Betty Neels*
Could Annis ever make Jake see that she had married him for love, and not on the rebound?

LOVE IS A FRENZY by *Charlotte Lamb*
Seventeen-year-old Nicky Hammond's devotion was touching, but Rachel couldn't possibly return it. Yet how could she convince his disapproving father Mark that she wasn't cradle-snatching — or worse?

THIS SIDE OF PARADISE by *Kay Thorpe*
Gina's so-called friend was after a man with money, so Gina couldn't really blame Ryan Barras when he got entirely the wrong idea about her . . .

A LAND CALLED DESERET by *Janet Dailey*
LaRaine had always been able to twist men round her finger but, as luck would have it, she fell in love with Travis McCrea — who had no time for her at all!

TANGLED SHADOWS by *Flora Kidd*
Kathryn could hardly refuse to return to her husband when she learned from his family that he had lost his memory in an accident — but would he remember what had destroyed the marriage in the first place?

THE PASSIONATE WINTER by *Carole Mortimer*
Piers Sinclair was her boy-friend's father: older, more sophisticated, far more experienced than she was. And so of course Leigh fell in love with him . . .

— all that's pleasurable in Romantic Reading!
Available October 1979

Also available this month
Four titles in our Mills & Boon
Classics Series
Specially chosen reissues of the best in Romantic Fiction

September's Titles are:

DARK ENEMY
by Anne Mather

Determined to revenge herself on Jason Wilde because of the way he had treated her sister, Nicola took a job with the oil company Jason worked for. To achieve her purpose, she determined to make him attracted to her. But things did not quite work out in the manner she expected.

MY HEART'S A DANCER
by Roberta Leigh

Melanie's marriage had ended before it had begun — but happily it was not long before she found herself in love once again. Yet even now happiness looked like eluding her, when her career as a ballet dancer began to come between her and the man she loved.

SECRET HEIRESS
by Eleanor Farnes

Young love is a pretty sight; but is it always strong and durable? Fiona's father had his doubts, and that was why he arranged for her to see a little of life outside her own small circle before becoming engaged to Guy. Would the experiment be successful, or might it lead her into real unhappiness?

THE PAGAN ISLAND
by Violet Winspear

In an effort to forget her grief over her beloved Dion's death, Hebe had gone to the lovely Greek island of Petra. There she met Nikos Stephanos, a man as different from Dion as he could possibly be. But a dark tragedy lay over Nikos's life. Would he bring tragedy to Hebe as well?

Mills & Boon Classics
— all that's great in Romantic Reading!

BUY THEM TODAY